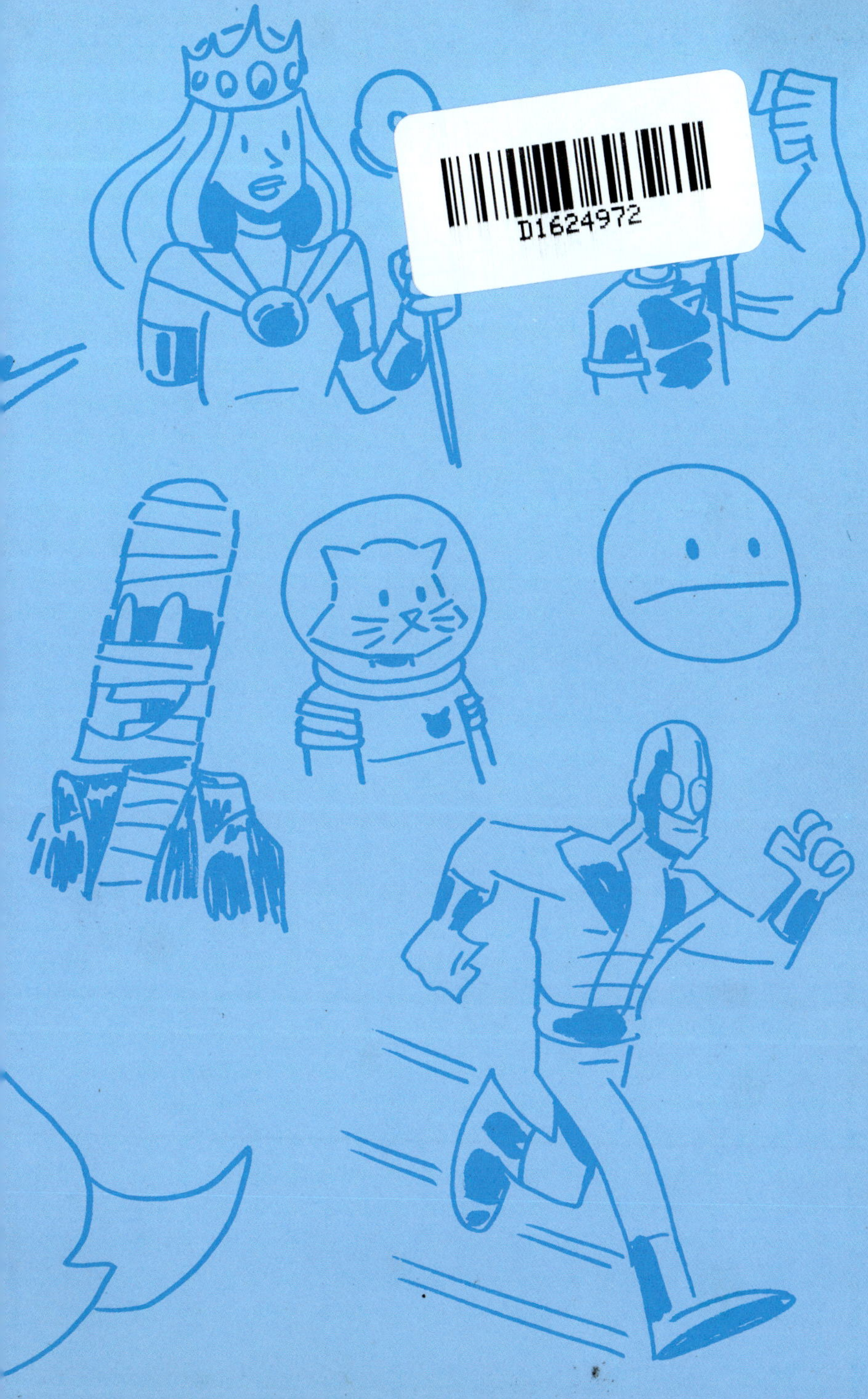

THE G-MAN™ SUPER JOURNAL

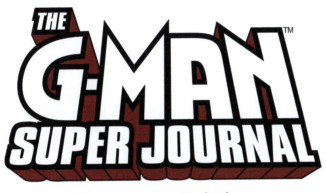

Awesome Origins

Other books by Chris Giarrusso

G-MAN: Learning to Fly
G-MAN: Cape Crisis
G-MAN: Coming Home

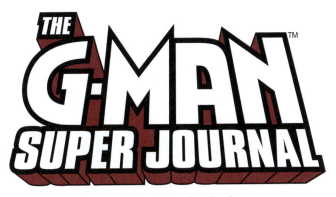

THE G-MAN SUPER JOURNAL™

Awesome Origins

Chris Giarrusso

Andrews McMeel Publishing

Kansas City · Sydney · London

THURSDAY

Yesterday, our English teacher, Mrs. Rosario, told us our new ongoing assignment will be to keep a journal. At first I thought that meant I would "keep" a journal the same way I "keep" my robots — on a bookshelf in my room.

But by "keep" a journal, she means we have to write in it on a regular basis, which is going to be significantly more effort than I had first imagined.

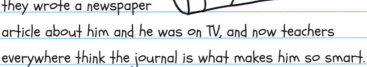

Apparently some smart kid in some other school has been keeping a journal, and they wrote a newspaper article about him and he was on TV, and now teachers everywhere think the journal is what makes him so smart.

So now we're all copying him by keeping our own journals in a desperate attempt to replicate his success.

Mrs. Rosario told us to bring in a journal book to start writing in today, and here we go. I can feel myself getting smarter already. She said we can write about whatever we want, but if we were stuck for ideas, she suggested writing a self-intro for our first journal entry — basically anything about ourselves. So I'll start with the question I'm asked most often...

You see, my friends all call me G-Man. It's a nickname. My real name is Michael G. So the nickname comes from my last name. People commonly assume the "G" is simply an initial. It's NOT. "G" is my ENTIRE last name.

Yes, I know it's weird. I've been told this many times. Although, you would think Jen Goodwell, of all people, would have a little more empathy and respect where my name is concerned, considering how sensitive SHE can be about names.

HEY, JENNY...

MY NAME ISN'T JENNY, IT'S JEN!!!

To the best of my knowledge, the whole "G" name began with my grandfather, who immigrated to the United States from Italy in 1893.

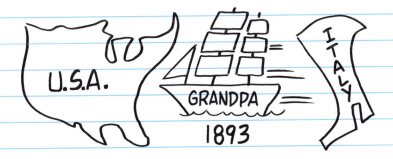

U.S.A.

GRANDPA 1893

ITALY

During his voyage across the Atlantic Ocean, most of the people on the boat died of an illness that mysteriously spared my grandfather. He was four years old and without any family when he arrived at Ellis Island.

My brother Dave says that story is just Grandpa telling tall tales. He says the stories of accidental name changes at Ellis Island are mostly untrue, and besides, according to that story, my grandfather would have to be over 120 years old, which he clearly is not. Most people usually assume the whole story is made up, but my grandfather's impossible age is not even the reason why.

THAT'S the part of my grandfather's story people can't believe. His FIRST name. The idea that two people could have the same name seems to transcend the boundaries of the imagination, even though we have two Jasons in our class.

I guess everyone assumes the name "Luigi" was just made up for that video game, but my grandfather was named Luigi WAY before video games were ever even invented!

So anyway... that's how I got my name and my nickname.

I think I'm off to a pretty brilliant start with this journal here, if you ask me. I wonder how long it will take for me to get into the newspaper.

Today, Mrs. Rosario suggested we write about somebody we admire. That's easy — Captain Thunderman!

Captain Thunderman standing on the steps of City Hall

Captain Thunderman is our city's greatest champion, which means he's the officially sanctioned superhero representative of our city.

He's super strong...

He's invulnerable...

Also he can fly, and he carries this awesome lightning bolt that shoots thunderblasts!

I like a lot of other superheroes, too, but Captain Thunderman is my favorite. Nobody really knows for sure where Captain Thunderman came from. My friends all have different theories. Billy thinks he's from another planet.

Eddie Delta thinks his powers were inherited through ancestry that traces directly back to Zeus, the ancient Greek god of thunder and sky.

Curtis heard that he was just an ordinary maintenance man for the utilities company, and he was caught in a freak accident during a routine inspection at the Lava Lords Volcano Energy Corporation's power plant.

Brian thinks he was part of a government experiment.

Those tend to be the same theories floating around for almost EVERY superhero, so nobody really knows for sure. But everybody agrees that Captain Thunderman is awesome, and we ALL want to be superheroes, too! Except for my math and science teacher, Mr. Leary.

Mr. Leary says superheroes just got lucky in getting superpowers, and they shouldn't be glorified for their dumb luck.

Mr. Leary is always saying we need to study and work hard to get a good education. And nobody really disagrees with him on that point. We DO study, and we DO work hard, and we DO get decent grades — he's the one grading us, so he should know this! But he just carries on and on about it all the time, pointing to his precious college diploma that he's so proud of.

We've seen it every one of the 653 times he's pointed it out.

MONDAY

Captain Thunderman battled Mister Mental this past weekend!

As you could probably guess, Mister Mental is a supervillain with mental powers that he can use to take over people's minds.

Mister Mental, Mad Master of Mental Manipulation

Mister Mental took psychic control of everyone at the big basketball game this Saturday and then just started helping himself to wallets and purses.

But Captain Thunderman was watching the game on TV, so he showed up and grabbed Mister Mental.

Captain Thunderman's helmet keeps him protected from psychic attacks, so Mister Mental used his powers to make people start jumping out of the bleachers. Captain Thunderman had to let go of Mister Mental to save those people, and Mister Mental escaped.

After that, there was a press conference where reporters kept asking Captain Thunderman variations on the exact same questions over and over for an hour. So the entire press conference really just amounted to this...

Captain Thunderman has caught Mister Mental before. Several times, actually. But Mister Mental keeps escaping from jail. They always think they've figured out some way to neutralize his mental powers, but it never works.

So a lot of people are critical of how Mister Mental has been dealt with in the past. My dad thinks he knows the perfect place to put him.

My brother Dave thinks everything related to Mister Mental is an elaborate hoax, and they just stage incidents like the one at the basketball game in order to scare people into buying those Mental Defense Helmets they advertise on TV.

Dave doesn't even believe Mister Mental actually HAS mental powers, but if he DID...

I think Dave has a point. I'm pretty sure Captain Thunderman's personal helmet works, but it probably uses super-advanced technology that only he has access to. I doubt they could manufacture working replicas of it for the current retail price of $99.99.

They do look pretty cool in the TV commercial though.

We were talking about Captain Thunderman's recent battle with Mister Mental today. Unfortunately, we were within earshot of Mr. Leary, who was compelled to go on another anti-superhero rant, saying for the 700th time that superheroes are just beneficiaries of happenstance who luck into their powers and use them for fame and endorsements.

Brian mentioned the Suntroopers because he is actually in basic training to join the Suntrooper Space Force! Becoming a Suntrooper has nothing to do with luck. It takes a lot of discipline and hard work before someone earns the right to wear a superpowered solar suit, and then their job is to protect the earth and the solar system! I don't think it's fair to suggest they don't work hard or that they are only protecting us for fame and endorsements.

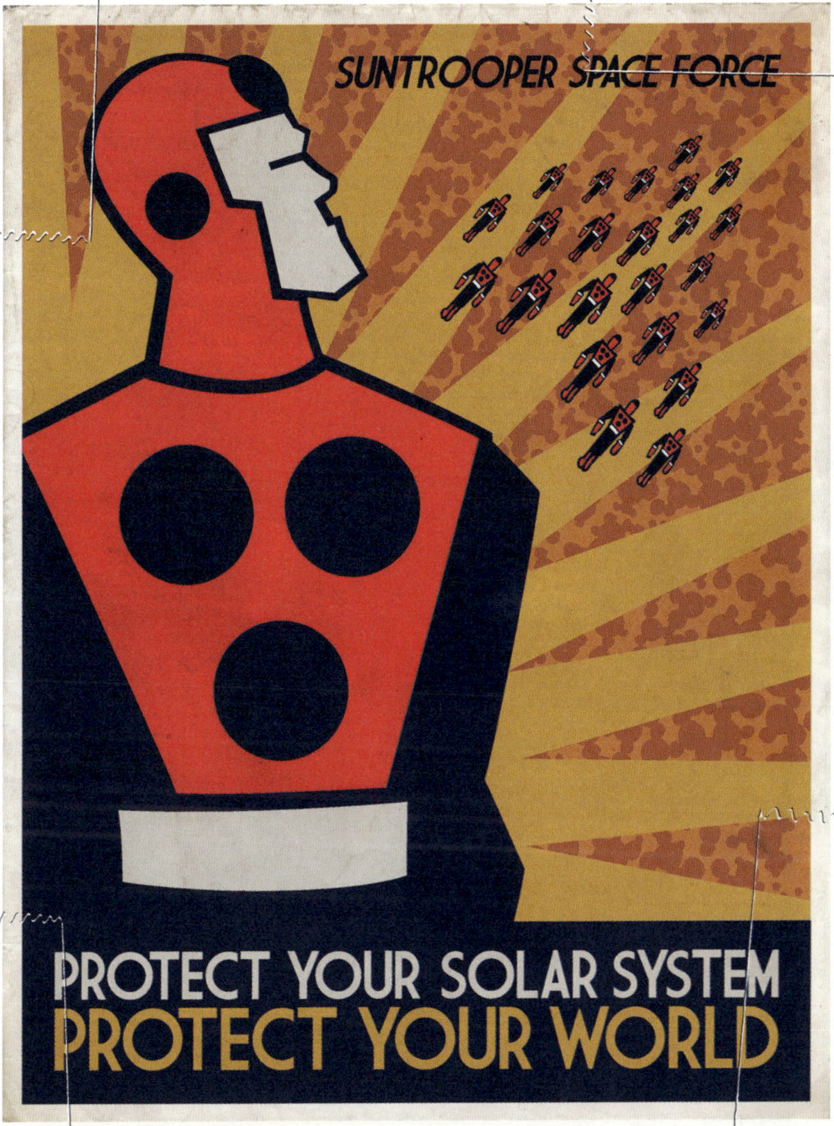
SUNTROOPER SPACE FORCE
PROTECT YOUR SOLAR SYSTEM
PROTECT YOUR WORLD

BRIAN'S FUTURE

AGAIN with the diploma!

I'm not sure why he's so fixated on whether or not Captain Thunderman has a diploma. For all we know, he DOES have one. But that's beside the point. Mr. Leary did not even answer Eddie Delta's question. That's probably because Mr. Leary doesn't want to acknowledge the fact that Eddie has superpowers and is a straight-A student, and he'll very likely earn a college diploma.

Eddie Delta's superpower is that he's always changing colors.

Some kids, like Tony Carboni, try to tease him about it...

Color changing isn't your typical glorified superhero power like flight or super strength... but it IS better than no powers at all. I'd happily take Eddie's superpowers if I could — it's not like superpowers are easy to come by. Plus, changing colors looks pretty cool, and the girls especially love it...

Eddie's mom says he was just born that way, but everyone speculates about his powers anyway...

Tony Carboni is the worst though. He's always so confrontational about everything, and he just doesn't let up.

It's nearly impossible to have a rational discussion with Tony. Eddie discovered it's often easier to just play along.

Eddie can turn any color he wants, and his power also affects his clothing, so he can effectively camouflage himself by blending into almost any background. He says patterns are trickier, but I saw him blend into a brick wall once.

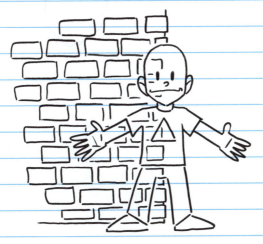

As with his clothing, Eddie can extend his power to affect whatever he touches, like his desk or even another person.

One time, he helped me skip a test I forgot to study for.

If Eddie is just relaxing and not trying to focus on his appearance, his colors gradually fluctuate around the color spectrum. But our gym teacher, Coach Oxbear, makes him hold his color whenever we're playing a team sport like basketball. He says the color shifting is an "unfair competitive advantage." That doesn't make sense to me, but maybe Coach thinks something like this will happen...

I think it technically ends up being a DISADVANTAGE for Eddie to hold one color. He has to split his focus between his color and the game, while the rest of us only have to focus on the game. But he's so good, it really doesn't make any difference.

Eddie is probably the best basketball player in our class, if not the whole school, even though he's smaller than most of us. He's perfected a fake-out maneuver called the jelly move. You think he's going one way, but suddenly he's gone the other way. In trying to reestablish your footing to keep up, your legs just collapse as if they have been turned to jelly.

So he's a great athlete, AND he's a straight-A student. He'll probably earn a college scholarship someday! The point is Eddie Delta has superpowers AND will earn a college diploma, no matter what Mr. Leary has to say about it. So there's no reason I shouldn't dream of having my own powers.

WEDNESDAY

I had to write a report on the life of an important figure in American history for social studies class. I picked Rick Adams, a little guy who volunteered for a top-secret experiment for the army during World War II.

Unfortunately, an enemy spy attempted to sabotage the experiment, and Rick's face was terribly scarred mid-transformation.

Otherwise, the experiment was successful, and Rick was transformed into a really big guy with huge muscles and a seemingly indestructible body.

The army wanted Rick to be their ultimate propaganda tool for boosting national morale — a living symbol of strength and freedom. Unfortunately, they didn't think that would be possible if people could see Rick's face. They thought his scars would remind people that war is actually dangerous and horrible. So they put a big helmet on Rick's head to hide his true face and replace it with an icon of undeniable optimism — the smiley face!

Then they put him in a colorful costume and gave him a big smiley face shield to carry into the battlefield. Thus was born G.I. Smiley, the Happy Hero!

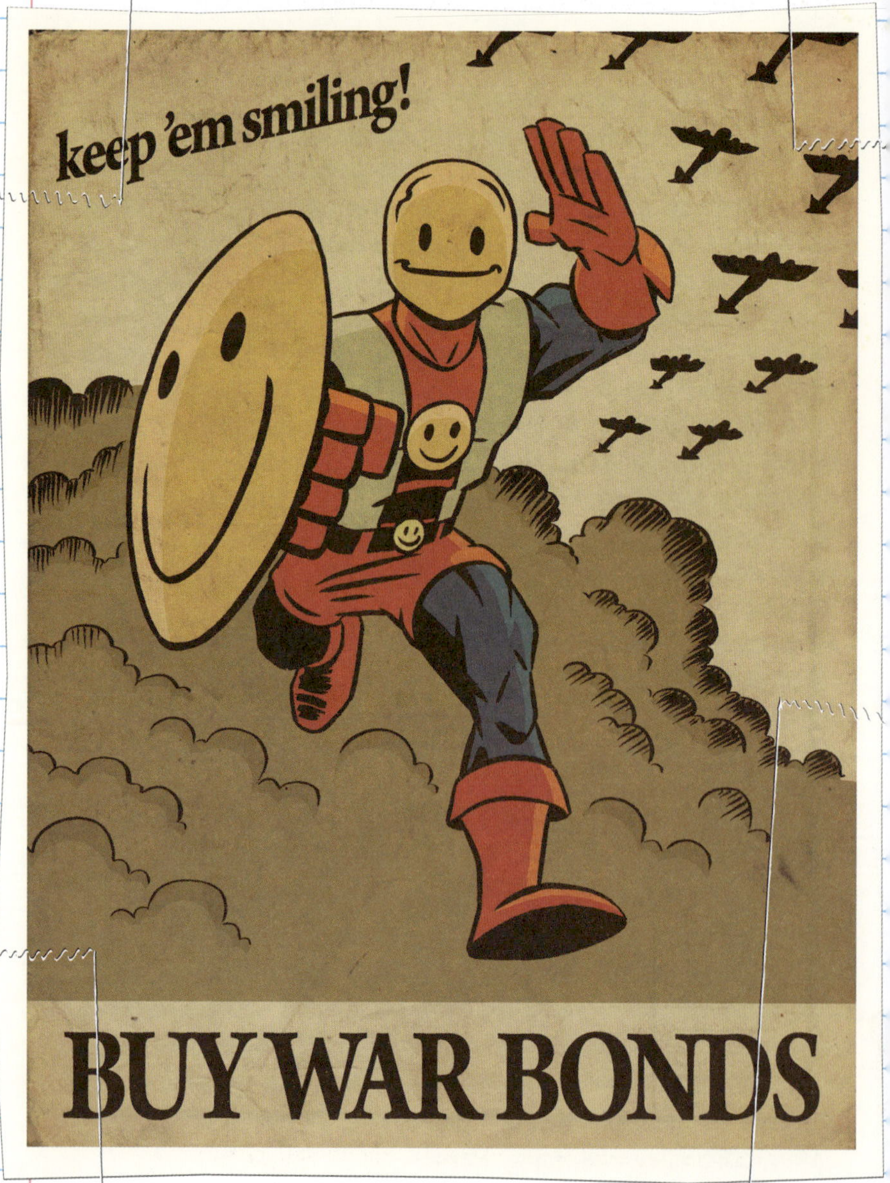
keep 'em smiling!
BUY WAR BONDS

A lot of people criticized the army's decision to dress up their most valuable soldier in an outfit that would make him so obviously visible to the enemy.

But that was the whole point. The army WANTED the enemy to focus on Happy Hero because he was INDESTRUCTIBLE! The enemy, eager to take down America's smiling symbol of freedom, focused all their efforts and wasted all their ammunition on Happy Hero.

This kept his fellow troops safer and allowed them to carry out missions relatively unchallenged.

Soon, the army succeeded in the creation of another superpowered soldier. He became Happy Hero's sidekick, known as Laughing Boy.

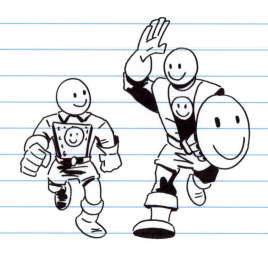

Unfortunately, Laughing Boy turned out not to be as indestructible as Happy Hero, and he died in battle.

Don't ask me why they never gave HIM a shield.

The army wanted to assign a new sidekick to Happy Hero right away, but Happy refused. He blamed himself for the

death of Laughing Boy, and he didn't want to see it
happen again.

So instead, the army created an entire elite special unit of
enhanced soldiers called the Laughing Boy Legion that fought
independently of Happy Hero.

What happened next is not entirely certain. There is currently
a Happy Hero fighting for justice today. Some say Rick
Adams is still the man in that uniform, alive and well as a

result of the secret formula granting him eternal youth and strength.

Others say Rick Adams finally met his end in the heart of an enemy's exploding nuclear bomb...

... and that the government has filled the Happy Hero uniform with a never-ending supply of enhanced soldiers over the course of the decades that followed.

Some say Rick Adams yet lives, but he retired from service in self-disgust after concluding that war and happiness cannot coexist.

NEVER AGAIN!

My brother Dave decided to help me with my report by using his computer photo art skills. I've never actually met Happy Hero, but it looks like we are good friends in this picture because Dave digitally inserted me into the scene like I belong there.

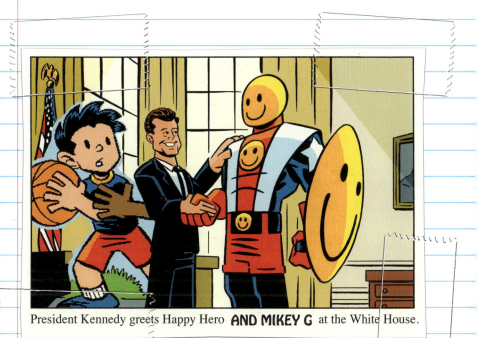

President Kennedy greets Happy Hero **AND MIKEY G** at the White House.

I totally got an A+ on the report, which Dave is now taking full credit for, as if his seamless computer photo manipulation amounted to the sum total of my report.

THURSDAY

Last night, super-famous pop singer Rita Lorita had a big concert in City Park, and the Color Guardians were attending guests of honor. The Color Guardians are a team of seven teenage princess superheroes, each one dressed in an individual color of the rainbow: red, orange, yellow, green, blue, indigo, and violet.

The Color Guardians pose triumphantly in front of the city skyline.

I always get indigo and violet mixed up, since they are basically both purple. The Color Guardians wear power gems on their vests and tiaras that give them enhanced strength, flight, and the ability to fire different colored power blasts.

Their leader is the Color Queen, who wields their entire spectrum of power and carries some sort of power scepter.

Color Queen stands at the steps of the city museum.

So Rita Lorita was onstage, and all of a sudden she started singing all kinds of swear words and calling the Color Guardians bad names!

33

Everyone thought it was just another outrageous stunt by a pop star for the sake of getting more attention. Color Queen flew to the stage and took away Rita's microphone so the audience wouldn't hear her bad language, but then Rita slapped Color Queen in the face! Color Queen looked stunned for a minute, and then she pointed her scepter at Rita like she was going to blast her!

It was Mister Mental all along! He took control of Rita's mind, and then Color Queen's mind, too! But then...

Color Queen was able to overcome Mister Mental's control! My guess is it was because of the power gemstones in her crown. Once he was revealed in the crowd, the Color Guardians dove in and grabbed him!

Or so they thought!

Mister Mental was able to temporarily fool them with one more mind trick as he made his escape.

Once they were sure Mister Mental was gone and nobody was hurt, the concert resumed, and everyone had a great time. The Color Guardians even danced onstage with Rita Lorita while she sang her #1 hit song, "Tippy Toe."

Yup. Those are pretty much ALL the words to the top song on the pop charts. I really hated that song the first time I heard it, but now I find myself singing it all the time in my head.

After the concert, Color Queen explained what happened at a press conference.

FRIDAY

Guess who came to school with one of those Captain
Thunderman Mental Defense Helmets today?

Tony Carboni!

After seeing that thing up close, I have to say my brother
Dave was right — there's no way that helmet can really
protect somebody from a psychic attack. The whole thing
is made out of cheap plastic. I can't believe anybody would
spend a hundred bucks on that. On second thought, I guess I
can when it's a guy who says stuff like this...

He usually says something like that when he's mad he can't get what he wants. Speaking of getting what he wants, Tony immediately tried to use his helmet as a bargaining chip.

Eddie doesn't really have any helmets at home.

I have to admit I REALLY wanted to try the helmet on.

Apparently, Tony was at the Rita Lorita concert, and his dad freaked out after the Mister Mental attack, so he bought one of those helmets for Tony. I did not think this was possible, but now Tony is acting like even MORE of a big shot.

I REALLY hope Mister Mental attacks our school immediately.

SUNDAY

Today we went to the mall because my mom said we needed new socks. I have a ton of socks already.

I don't get it. Sometimes kids tease me at school for wearing a shirt or a jacket or pants or sneakers that aren't cool. You know... things people can SEE. And THAT can be embarrassing...

But nobody can see my socks. I don't imagine anybody would care if they discovered there WERE holes in them. Maybe my mom thinks this is what happens at school...

The holes are not even that big. I think my mom is blowing this whole sock situation way out of proportion. On this point, my brother Dave and I agree. We believe the sock money would be better spent on more important things.

When we got to the mall, there was a big crowd at one of

the kiosks. There was a big sale on Mental Defense Helmets
for half off!

Fifty bucks is still a total rip-off, but people were jumping
all over each other to buy them. Dave and I could not believe
those suckers lining up to waste their money on those
things! My mom saw somebody she knew waiting in line...

My mom said we were being rude.

We made our way over to the food court for some lunch, where there seemed to be yet another strange commotion. There was a big circle of people, everyone staring at a guy eating a soft pretzel at one of the tables. That guy was Mister Mental!

He must have been there long enough for word to spread, because just then, this group of five teenagers wearing Mental Defense Helmets charged past us and headed right at him like they were going to fight him. They thought they were going to be heroes, but instead...

And since we were standing behind them, we also got hit with the mental whammy! We could feel Mister Mental's powers affecting us!

Then the teenagers, who recieved the full brunt of the attack, fell down unconscious. We were released from the effects unharmed, probably because we were farther away. Mister Mental didn't do anything else to anybody. He just finished his pretzel and left. Then everyone immediately swarmed the helmet kiosk to demand their money back.

Afterward, my mom was really worried about Dave and me. She said we had gone through a traumatic experience. She insisted we were really upset and said she would buy us each one action figure. I was maybe a little upset that Dave criticized my chicken skills, but otherwise we were fine. We DID want action figures, though, so we seized that opportunity before the topic of socks could be revisited.

Meanwhile, my mom noticed a sale on picture frames, and she started loading up. She does this pretty much EVERY time there's a sale on frames. Over time, my mom has accumulated boxes and boxes of picture frames that sit in the basement patiently waiting for the day when she will unite them with actual pictures — a day that will likely never come. At this point, I think the frames in our house may actually outnumber the photos.

Given the circumstances of our recent "traumatic experience," I thought maybe we could subtly steer my mom into letting us get TWO action figures each, instead of spending money on more picture frames we don't need.

I don't think there's any question that an action figure is WAY better than a picture frame, but Dave was right. Even though those picture frames were never going to serve any purpose, it was best not to cause a fuss. I returned my focus to searching out the best action figure. The choice was obvious. Of course I wanted my favorite superhero, Captain Thunderman!

But Dave wanted a Captain Thunderman, too. He kept telling me I should get a different hero so that we could have "team-up adventures," and two Captain Thunderman figures wouldn't be as fun. Plus, my mom said she wasn't going to buy two of the same toy, so I ended up getting a Captain Rocketron figure. When we got home, our "team-up adventures" unfolded. It was a lot of "fun."

Later, footage of the Mister Mental food court incident was all over the news. The news people were slamming Captain Thunderman for endorsing those helmets when they only put people in danger.

At a press conference, Captain Thunderman said he had agreed to selling toy helmets for $9.99 to raise money for funding various city projects. Without permission from Captain Thunderman or the city, the company that manufactured the helmets decided they could turn a huge profit by marketing them as a security measure against Mister Mental and charging ten times the original price.

MONDAY

Today was awesome! Things got off to a great start the second I got on the bus and saw Tony Carboni sitting there.

What then commenced was possibly the greatest bus ride of all time...

On any other day, Tony would have had an entire day's worth of teasing rightfully in store for him. But lucky for Tony, everyone forgot all about him and his worthless helmet the second we saw Billy. Billy was sporting a significantly different look than he normally does.

BILLY LAST WEEK
BILLY TODAY

Billy showed up at school today in an AWESOME SUPERHERO COSTUME with REAL SUPERPOWERS! Some of the kids think he's just dressed up and he doesn't really have powers, but everyone on my bus saw Billy flying around outside before school started!

WOW, BILLY IS FLYING!
HE IS A COOL DUDE!

He looks AWESOME. With those horns and wings, he looks a lot like the Cyber Demon of Tech City and the Knight Demon from Camelot City...

Cyber Demon glides across the skies of Tech City.

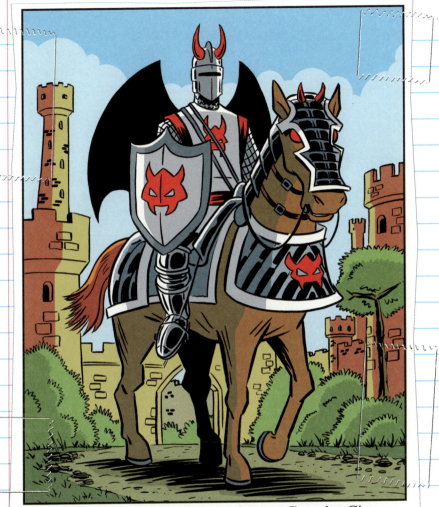

The mysterious Knight Demon departs Camelot City.

So now everyone's referring to Billy as "Billy Demon"!

I HAVE to learn how Billy made his wings so I can make a pair of my OWN! He must have figured out some way to stretch lightweight latex or nylon over a mechanical skeletal structure that he can manipulate with his shoulder blades and back muscles.

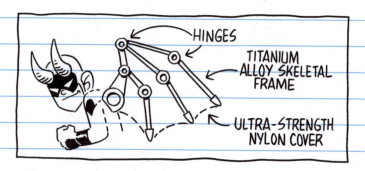

HINGES

TITANIUM ALLOY SKELETAL FRAME

ULTRA-STRENGTH NYLON COVER

I always suspected such a thing might be possible, but I figured it would be too complicated or expensive. Now I MUST get to the bottom of this!

After all, I've wanted superpowers forever, and if I had to pick ONE superpower, I would DEFINITELY pick flying! My friend Jeff says he wouldn't want to fly because he's afraid of heights, but that makes NO SENSE. First of all, EVERYONE is afraid of heights, or more specifically, FALLING FROM heights (see diagram of awesome, below).

AWESOME

NOT AWESOME

I agree it's scary to be up somewhere high where you might fall. That's just the natural human instinct for survival. But if you can FLY, then there is no longer any danger of falling, so there is no reason to be afraid of heights! I've tried to explain this to Jeff, but he still insists he has a fear of heights. I think he's just trying to sound interesting by being different. And it actually works.

Anyway, I just can't wait to talk to Billy about his costume later! We're really good friends, so I think he'll probably let me try out his wings!

Billy won't let me try out his wings. But I was kind of expecting that after the way recess unfolded yesterday.

I thought I was desperate to try the wings, but all the other kids went CRAZY! I wouldn't want to let those maniacs touch my brand-new wings either if I were Billy! Eventually, the kids got tired of chasing him, and everyone seemed to accept the fact that Billy wasn't going to let anyone wear his wings.

Except for Tony Carboni, of course.

As if that dumb helmet wasn't garbage enough, Tony offered
an even more worthless currency.

The girls seemed to really like the wings, too.

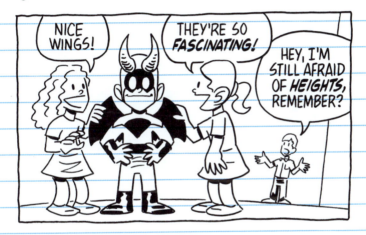

Later, Billy told me the wings are really expensive and tricky
to operate, and anybody else besides him would probably
break them because they won't know what they're doing,
and he doesn't want some idiot breaking his expensive wings.
Also, his dad doesn't want to get sued if a kid gets hurt. I
hadn't considered any of that, but it's understandable. I still
need to discuss how he made them though. Maybe I can
make my own wings.

I woke up sick this morning. Sore throat, chills, and aches all over my body. My mom took my temperature and said I needed to stay home from school.

Dave was sick yesterday with the exact same bug. It is not at all surprising that I got sick from his germs, and Dave is more than smart enough to understand this. He KNOWS I'm not faking.

His REAL concern is the video games. There is nothing in the world more important to my brother than video games, and a fundamental part of his gaming life is to perpetually blame ME for breaking the controllers.

This is how Dave plays video games...

This is how I play video games...

See how I'm not even in those panels? That's because I
don't even play. So, how am I blamed for breaking controllers
I never touch? In the early days, when we first got our
video game system, I DID play. I was excited to play. I would
wait quietly and patiently for my turn.

When Dave finally allowed me a turn at playing, he would blast music, scream, and bang on things to distract me.

It was a difficult set of circumstances under which to concentrate on games that required focus and finely tuned hand-eye coordination. My turns were brief.

Over time, after a certain amount of gaming...

... the controllers would mysteriously stop working.

I tried to protest, but my mom just said I was being "defensive." I don't know what other kind of stance to take when I'm trying to defend myself, but I've learned that when someone accuses you of being defensive, that means they are not going to listen to anything you say.

This gave Dave exclusive use of the video games. I was banned. However, Dave would occasionally lift the ban under the false pretense that he was bored playing by himself and wanted a "real challenge." In reality, he lifted the ban for two reasons.

Reason #1:

Dave simply enjoys taunting and humiliating me. Denying me any degree of fun adds an extra dynamic to the games and enhances his ability to enjoy them. Perhaps in that sense, it IS fair to consider this particular variation of gaming a unique "challenge," although it doesn't seem very challenging for Dave at all. As a result of his masterful skills, I have never had fun playing a video game.

But there was a BIGGER reason Dave would periodically lift my ban.

Reason #2:

Dave would invite me to play only AFTER he broke the controllers. Then he conveniently blamed ME for the controllers not working. It took me a while to figure out his ruse, but my mom will be forever blind to my brother's cunning tricks.

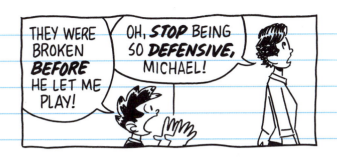

With my mom unwilling to listen, I had no other choice but to take matters into my own hands. I was backed into a corner, desperate, ready to do the unthinkable. The next time Dave put me in this position, I was forced to take EXTREME measures...

Dave was dumbfounded. He never anticipated the day would come when I wouldn't jump at the chance to play a video game. It never occurred to him that by systematically spoiling every video game experience I've ever had, he would be responsible for destroying any interest I once had in playing. He'd have been proud of himself if it hadn't backfired on him so badly.

But backfire, it did. It's nearly impossible for him to blame me for broken controls when I never touch them. So the reason he kicked up a fuss about me staying home this morning was to make my mom fully aware I was going to be all alone with the video games, setting up the opportunity to blame me for breaking the controllers again. But I was onto his scheme, and I thwarted it immediately.

A rare victory for me.

Now I would definitely rather not be sick, but I WAS still happy to be alone for the day. This meant I could watch whatever I wanted on TV without Dave changing the channels or without my parents turning the TV off. Just me on the couch under the magic blanket watching cartoons and sitcoms.

The magic blanket is just this blanket that we use whenever somebody gets sick, sort of as a superstition. It started with my grandfather. He had the blanket with him on the boat when he first came to this country, and since so many people got sick and died on that boat, he called the blanket his good luck charm — the magic blanket that kept him alive. Now, it's the comfortable blanket that keeps me warm while I watch a two-hour block of the old sitcom "Greene House" on the retro channel.

My FAVORITE episode was on — the one guest starring COOL WRAPS! Cool Wraps is another one of my favorite superheroes. He's an old Egyptian mummy burdened with an ancient curse that gives him long life and superpowers. But instead of being an evil monster (like SOME mummies), he decided he might as well make lots of friends and have fun and help people with his superpowers! That episode of "Greene House" is an all-time television classic!

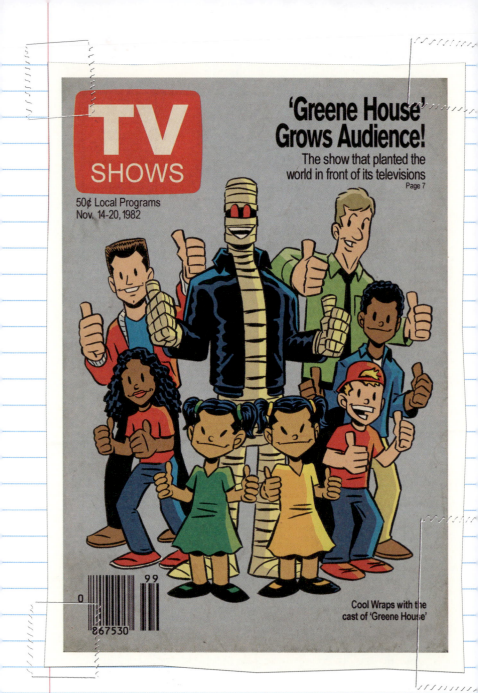

Cool Wraps with the cast of 'Greene House'

66

Next up was the classic bike episode (I guess all episodes of "Greene House" are classics). I fell asleep in the middle of that one and ended up having a weird fever dream that I gave Helen and Curly Greene a ride home on my bike.

I was riding my bike on the water across the lake to their house, and then Helen jumped off to go swimming. When I got to the Greene House with Curly, he let all the air out of my tires and said, "Thanks for NOTHIN'!" Then Mr. Greene came outside and hung my bike from a tree branch and told me to get lost. Which reminds me of something Dave once told me.

NOBODY WANTS
TO HEAR
ABOUT YOUR
STUPID
DREAMS.

After everybody came home tonight, I overheard Dave talking to my mom.

Car accident?

Very clever. Dave dodged the blame again, but at least THIS time I've managed to avoid any remote chance of this being considered MY fault.

I guess my earlier declaration of victory was premature.

FRIDAY

Ever since Billy got his demon suit, everyone's been talking about superheroes and superpowers more than ever before.

I guess Mr. Leary had more than he could take of our civilized and imaginative discussions, because he told us we need to get over our "childish power fantasies." But THAT was more than I could take of Mr. Leary. I'm tired of the way he condescendingly trivializes our interest in superpowers as if there's something wrong with it.

Wow, what a great attitude! I thought he was supposed to encourage us to IMPROVE ourselves. I guess I should be glad he's just my teacher and not my DOCTOR...

... or a RESTAURANT OWNER...

... or a FIREMAN...

At the end of class, Mr. Leary assigned homework and said we needed to study for tomorrow's quiz. I felt compelled to point out that homework and studying are only going to make our brains faster, stronger, and better, which would directly contradict Mr. Leary's assertion that we should be happy with ourselves the way we are.

Mr. Leary felt compelled to give me an after-school detention.

The worst part of detention is that you have to write a letter to your parents explaining why you got a detention. It's like being forced to tell on yourself. But it's even more difficult in a situation like mine where you haven't actually done anything wrong. The explanation just won't sound very convincing. So I wrote:

> Dear Mom and Dad,
> I was assigned a detention today because I exposed my math and science teacher Mr. Leary for the true hypocrite that he is in front of the whole class by using his own words against him, and his ego was too fragile to handle such a crushing defeat at the hands of a student.

I would have been happy to show my parents that letter, but I forgot Mr. Leary would have to approve it first.

Can you believe he made me rewrite it? I bet you are as shocked as I was. So I came up with this:

Dear Mom and Dad,

I was assigned a detention today because Mr. Leary
is so thoroughly jealous of superheroes, he simply
cannot handle being in earshot of a conversation
about one. I think he is extra jealous lately because
Billy recently got an awesome flying demon suit.

I thought that one was pretty good, but Mr. Leary took
away my recess for Monday after he read it. After much
brainstorming, I finally determined the key to an acceptable
letter would be to deemphasize Mr. Leary's role in the
incident:

Dear Mom and Dad,

I was assigned a detention today because I
want to be a superhero. I think it would be fun to
have superpowers, but I also like that superheroes
use their powers to help people. I think
superheroes can inspire us all to be better people
whether we have superpowers or not, and I want to
improve myself. But Mr. Leary doesn't like
superpowers, and he says I should be happy with
myself the way I am. I told Mr. Leary that studying
and getting smarter was like getting a superpower,
and that's why he assigned me a detention.

Surprisingly, Mr. Leary approved it. Now all I had to do was get my mom to sign it.

My mom won't sign my letter. She doesn't believe a teacher would give me a detention for saying being smart is like having a superpower. So she got mad at me for lying (which I wasn't), and then my dad walked in to find her yelling at me. He was in no mood to listen to the intricate chain of events that led to my predicament, nor do I believe he would have sympathized. He just jumped straight to one of his three perpetual angry dad commands...

The other two perpetual angry dad commands are...

 AND

Good manners are very important to my dad.

My brother Dave said Mr. Leary is just one of those awful teachers with a Napoleon complex. I guess that means Napoleon must have behaved like this...

Brian came to school looking a little bit different today...

Last night, Brian completed basic training for the Suntrooper Space Force! He's now an official Suntrooper, and from now on, he'll be wearing his solar suit to school! He looks awesome! We're all calling him "Sunny" now because Junior Suntrooper Agents are commonly referred to as Sunny Boys and Sunny Girls.

As I write this, Sunny is outside flying around for recess. Since I lost my recess during my detention last Friday, I'm stuck in Mr. Leary's classroom. Even worse, Mr. Leary gave me another detention because I didn't get Friday's detention letter signed! At least he's letting me write in my journal since it's schoolwork, but he keeps looking over my shoulder to see what I'm writing, which is pretty annoying. I swear the only time he's not hovering over me is when he goes to the teachers' lounge for a coffee refill.

Anyway, as I was saying, Sunny's solar suit enables him to fly not only on earth, but it generates an energy field around him that let's him fly in SPACE! The suit is powered by stored solar energy that comes from solar cells covering the vest, boots, and arm gauntlets. The arm gauntlets also fire solar blasts of varying intensity.

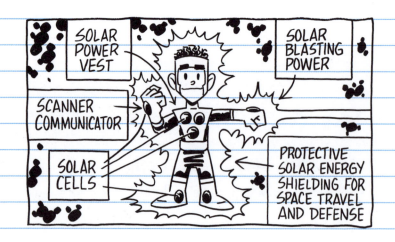

The Suntrooper Space Force protects our planet and solar system from extraterrestrial threats, like when the Cat People of the Lyran Star System attempted to invade Earth.

Every once in a while, an asteroid will come around that is on a collision course with Earth. If an asteroid were to impact our planetary surface, it could end all life on Earth as we know it. Lucky for us, the Suntrooper Space Force is always on the lookout, and they destroy a dozen or so asteroids each week that would otherwise result in impacts of apocalyptic proportion.

Scientists say an asteroid DID hit Earth millions of years ago and is responsible for the extinction of the dinosaurs. But some believe the dinosaurs got into a dinosaur spaceship and left the planet before the asteroid could hit.

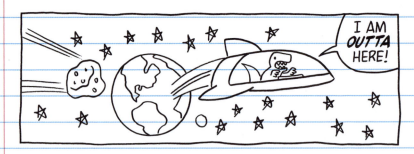

Others think they went underground and survived all this time and evolved into dragons.

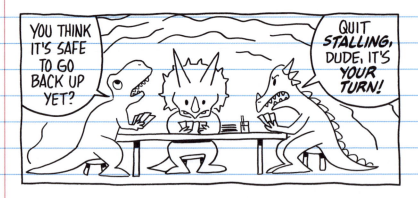

Regardless of what really happened to the dinosaurs, everyone agrees that asteroid collisions with Earth would be bad, and it's good that we have the Suntrooper Space Force protecting us.

I really wish I could wear Sunny's solar suit! It would be so awesome to fly and shoot solar blasts and feel what it would be like to be a real superhero! I'm sure he'd let me if he could, but he would get in big trouble if he let anybody else wear his solar suit. The Suntroopers have a MAJOR rule against it. It's a pretty big deal, and Sunny even made a class announcement about it at the beginning of the day. Immediately, he found himself having THIS conversation...

Tony doesn't understand sarcasm.

But as I look out the window right now, it appears as if

Tony isn't the only one trying to get Sunny to bend the rule.

Mr. Leary just came over and yelled at me for drawing pictures. He says a journal is supposed to be full of WRITING, not PICTURES. I told him he can talk to Mrs. Rosario about it, since SHE'S my teacher who's having us keep journals.

He keeps hovering over me with his coffee breath (he drinks maybe twenty cups a day) right in my face so he can read what I'm writing. Now he's yelling at me for writing about how he's yelling at me. If this is making him mad, he better not read what I wrote about him Friday.

Okay, so after I wrote that last sentence, Mr. Leary snatched my journal and started paging through everything I wrote about him. Then he dragged me to Mrs. Rosario's classroom to let her know what I'd been doing. I thought I was going to lose recess for the rest of the year, but Mrs. Rosario said that my journal is supposed to be for private self-expression. I couldn't BELIEVE it! Usually, teachers just gang up against you, but Mrs. Rosario was DEFENDING me!

Then Mr. Leary pointed out the pictures I was drawing and said it wasn't REAL writing, and I should be able to express myself in words alone, and it demonstrated laziness and a lack of intelligence.

So I opened up the science book we use in Mr. Leary's class, and I pointed out that in addition to the words, the book was filled with diagrams and charts and models and maps and photographs.

I said it demonstrated that whoever uses that science book to teach us must be lazy and lacking in intelligence because they should be able to explain things with words alone.

Guess who lost their recess again for tomorrow? The answer is me. Mr. Leary was extra mad this time because Mrs. Rosario laughed, and I could tell she was trying not to. I was surprised he didn't also assign me another detention, but I think Mrs. Rosario's presence kept him from going overboard. It would be difficult for him to exaggerate my offense or justify further punishment with a sensible adult witness there to corroborate my side of the story...

But then I realized it really didn't matter one way or the other, because it turns out my detention situation is ALREADY a WORST-CASE SCENARIO! My mom still thinks I was lying about my first detention, and as long as she does, I will remain trapped in an INFINITE DETENTION LOOP!!!

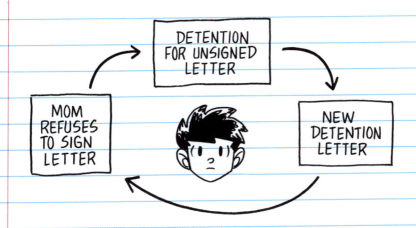

And I can't even make use of my detention time to write in my journal. Mr. Leary placed the restriction on me after Mrs. Rosario made it clear I can write and draw whatever I want.

Today we had gym class. Ordinarily I like gym class, but after two days of missed recess and after-school detention, I was REALLY looking forward to running around in gym like never before. But nothing could have prepared me for what turned out to be the most EPIC gym class of all time.

To start, our gym teacher, Coach Oxbear, said that Sunny and Billy had to leave their superhero costumes in their lockers because their suits would give them an unfair competitive advantage. Then, after we changed into our gym clothes, Coach Oxbear called attendance, and Tony Carboni was missing. I knew he wasn't absent from school. I had just seen him earlier in the day talking to Billy.

So Coach Oxbear went over to the locker room doorway and shouted for Tony to hurry up and come out. Tony came out... and he sure came out in a HURRY!

Tony had broken into Sunny's locker and put on his solar suit! He flew around the gym, and Coach yelled at him to come down, but this time he did not obey Coach's commands. Soon, everyone was yelling. Sunny was furious.

Then Tony tried the solar blaster.

I didn't know you could get a technical foul when there isn't a game being played, but I also never saw anybody so flagrantly disrespect Coach before. Coach said Tony had five seconds to come down and remove the solar suit willingly, or else they would have to do things the hard way. Tony laughed at him and kept flying around.

To be honest, I was glad Tony continued his disobedience, because I wanted to see what the "hard way" was going to be. See, Coach Oxbear is superhumanly strong and tough.

Elementary school gym coach and college physics professor Oxbear lends a hand with bus wheel repair.

We don't know exactly where he came from, but he appears to be part ox and part polar bear. Billy thinks he's from another planet...

Curtis thinks he was a regular human who took part in a secret government experiment....

Eddie thinks he's genetically related to the legendary Minotaur of the ancient Greeks...

GREAT GREAT GREAT GREAT GREAT GREAT GREAT GREAT GRANDPA

Whatever the case, I think Coach Oxbear is tough enough to fight a Suntrooper. I was hoping with all my might that Tony would fly low enough for Coach to grab him. But then, out of nowhere...

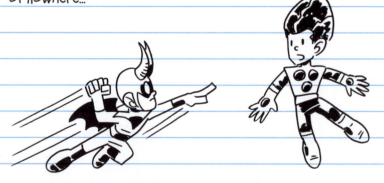

In the commotion, nobody noticed Billy had snuck back to the locker room to put on his demon suit. When he came streaking out in full demon—attack mode, everyone was sure

we were about to witness a real live super battle right
there in the gym! But Coach Oxbear told Billy to back off,
and as Billy started to come back down, Tony took a major
cheap shot!

Billy fell to the ground. For a second, we thought he was
dead! But his reinforced demon suit must have absorbed
most of the blast, because Billy sprang right back up and
charged at Tony again. You could totally see Tony's expression
change from bullying confidence to petrified fear. He even put
his hands up to try to protect himself. But before Billy could
lay a hand on Tony...

... a Senior Suntrooper Agent burst into the gym and put a halt to the fight! It turns out the Suntrooper Space Force tracks every active solar suit in case any Suntrooper winds up in an emergency situation that requires backup assistance. They received an alert as soon as Sunny's suit registered Tony's unsanctioned biosignature. The Senior Suntrooper Agent deactivated Sunny's suit, and they called Tony's dad to come in immediately. Tony messed up BIG TIME!

When Tony's dad arrived, he pulled out his wallet. I thought he was going to pay for the broken backboard, but he had something else in mind...

I was hoping the Suntrooper would blast Tony and his dad, but she didn't. Instead, she calmly explained the suits are not for sale, and the only way Tony could earn a suit would be through the Junior Suntrooper training program. This would be the same three-month program Sunny had just graduated from. I thought Tony's stunt should have been enough to earn him a lifetime ban from training program consideration, so I guess Tony is lucky I'm not in charge of the Suntrooper Space Force. But maybe she figured Tony wouldn't have the necessary discipline for the training program anyway. To enroll in the training program, first you have to pass the Suntrooper tryouts, which are a combination of academic and physical fitness testing.

FINALLY! This was my BIG CHANCE to become a real superhero! I signed up for tryouts immediately. Pretty much EVERYBODY signed up. Except for Jeff and Billy...

And there were a couple of other notable exceptions as well...

It appears that Jeff's charm is working again, though perhaps not quite as well as he'd like.

For the rest of the day, everyone was talking about joining the Suntrooper Space Force. I shared in the excitement, fantasizing about what I could do with a solar suit.

But that fantasy only caused my excitement level to plummet, as the thought of Mr. Leary brought the harsh reality of my infinite detention loop back into clear focus. If I can't break the loop, I won't be able to participate in the Suntrooper tryouts! I'll be stuck in Mr. Leary's classroom! I asked Mr. Leary if there was a limit to the number of detentions I could serve for a single offense, hoping the loop wasn't as infinite as it appeared.

He mocks me. OF COURSE there is something he COULD do. He makes up the rules. He COULD let me off the hook anytime. He just doesn't WANT to. I'm sure he is taking extra delight in keeping the Suntrooper opportunity out of my reach because he knows how badly I want to become a superhero.

I told him my mom has seen the letter and she won't sign it, but he refuses to take me seriously. He even started teasing me in front of Mrs. Rosario when she walked in.

When I got home, I tried to get my detention letter signed again.

Getting in trouble for saying that being smart is like having a superpower makes no sense to my mom. And to be fair, it shouldn't. On the other hand, getting punished for fighting

DOES make sense. Case in point, the last time I had a detention, it was for fighting. It wasn't actually a REAL fight, but at least it makes sense as something to get in trouble for. You see, Curtis and I were engaging in a test of strength during recess.

We had recess indoors that day. During our battle, Curtis tripped, and the resultant momentum carried the both of us tumbling into Jen Goodwell's desk, knocking me, Curtis, the desk, and the chair to the floor.

Mrs. Rosario thought Curtis and I were fighting, and she gave us both a detention. However, she did comment on how mature we both were about shaking hands afterward, so we let her think we were mature instead of explaining it was a strength competition gone awry. We figured it would have been a detention either way, and at least this way she had a certain measure of respect for us.

Realizing my mom was a lost cause, I tried asking my dad to sign the letter when he was in an approachable mood. Unfortunately, my mom was onto my scheme, and she quickly nullified that option.

Finally, I asked my brother Dave for advice.

There doesn't seem to be any way out of this.

WEDNESDAY

I returned to recess today, but it was not the glorious return it should have been. The dark cloud of the infinite detention loop cast a cold shadow upon every moment, a shadow made ever colder in contrast to the beaming sunshine of the enthusiastic Suntrooper discussion that was carrying on across the playground.

I sat and pondered my fate. All I ever wanted was to become a superhero. Is that asking too much? I know that superpowers are often a random thing to come by, but here was an opportunity I could WORK for... except the opportunity was now dangling just beyond my reach!

Eventually, they stopped giving me a hard time and started helping me brainstorm ways to defeat the infinite detention loop.

The loophole Curtis suggested would work as follows: If I could get another detention for doing something REALLY bad, then the new detention letter could reflect that new misbehavior. In turn, my mom would find this new count of misbehavior to be a credible reason for getting a detention, and she'd finally sign the letter!

So it was just a matter of figuring out exactly how to misbehave in front of Mr. Leary to instigate a detention. We came up with several detention-instigation plans.

I tried the simplest idea first, right after recess. Our next class was math with Mr. Leary. I took my time getting there so I would be undeniably late. I walked in expecting this...

But what happened instead was...

Unfortunately, I wasn't punished for being late. Mr. Leary seemed to take enough delight in the idea that I wouldn't have enough time to take the quiz. But that didn't matter because I still managed to finish the quiz (which I ACED, by the way) with time to spare.

Then I realized this was an opportunity to initiate another detention-instigation plan: cheating! I leaned over in my chair as far as I could to appear as suspicious as possible.

That was it? "Eyes on your own paper"? He must have noticed I was finished already and not really cheating. But because Mr. Leary had already seen me leaning, Jen decided this would be the perfect time to initiate my least favorite of the detention-instigation plans.

Surely, there would be no tolerance for a mid-class make-out attempt! Mr. Leary asked me if Jen's claim was true.

But Mr. Leary just sighed and said...

I couldn't understand why this guy who hates me wasn't getting upset over any of this. I was zero for three and running out of ideas!

I had one more trick up my sleeve... it was the most extreme of the detention-instigation plans we had devised. Curtis came up with this plan, and his participation was key. As our quizzes were handed forward for Mr. Leary to collect from the front row, I looked over at Curtis and Billy who looked back at me in silent agreement — NOW was the time to act!

I got up out of my chair and walked over to Curtis's desk. With Mr. Leary positioned behind me, I cocked my arm way back and took a big, arcing, open-handed swing at Curtis.

THIS WAS CURTIS'S IDEA, AND I DID NOT REALLY HIT HIM.

Curtis figured since we'd gotten detention for fighting in the past, this stunt would definitely be detention worthy. I safely missed Curtis by a few inches, and he leapt out of his seat, but from Mr. Leary's vantage point, it would have looked like I had connected. Billy, positioned behind Curtis, clapped his hands together under his desk with perfect timing so it sounded like the clap was generated from my hand slapping Curtis in the face.

The class let out an audible gasp. Everyone in the class was certain I had just knocked Curtis out of his chair for no reason. We fooled 'em ALL! That is, all but one notable, annoying exception...

Mr. Leary was onto us the whole time. Overcome with frustration, I instantly and involuntarily devised and initiated a new detention-instigation plan.

That DID get me in trouble, but not a detention. Instead, I lost my recess for tomorrow. I was so fixated on earning a detention, I had temporarily forgotten that losing recess was even a risk. Total backfire.

After school, I told my brother Dave everything about the formulation and subsequent failure of the detention-instigation plans, and how I was puzzled by my lack of punishment. Dave offered the following insight...

Dave stopped being a jerk for a few minutes and explained I had to understand the psychology of Mr. Leary. He pointed out that all of the bad things I did today were at the expense of other people, not Mr. Leary. The only stuff that ever got him angry was when I challenged something he said in class or mocked him in my journal. Dave said if I really wanted a detention, minor misbehavior wouldn't be enough. I would have to attack Mr. Leary directly.

SMACK!

No, not like that! That's just a drawing for private self-expression to vent my frustration! I would never do that for real!

I have a much better plan in mind.

FRIDAY

Today, I initiated my master detention-instigation plan
at the end of math class. Mr. Leary had given us the last
five minutes of class to silently work on our homework
assignment, and he was occupied with adjusting the projector
equipment after showing us a slideshow. All was calm.

I got out of my chair, walked behind Mr. Leary's momentarily
abandoned desk, and removed his diploma from the wall.

That alone was enough to get everyone's attention. There
was a stunned silence. Everyone knew I had just crossed a

huge line. It was one of those moments where everything seemed like it was happening in slow motion, almost like I was watching myself from the outside.

I looked up to see Mr. Leary staring back at me in shock, motionless like a deer caught in headlights, paralyzed not only by the audacity of what I had just done, but also by what we both knew I was about to do.

Smashing the diploma frame snapped Mr. Leary out of his paralysis stance. He bounded toward me in a rage, but was too late to prevent the inevitable...

I'm pretty sure I finally made Mr. Leary mad. To say he yelled at me is an understatement. It was like getting crushed by an avalanche of angry words.

I definitely heard the key word, "detention," but he was also sending me to the principal's office. I was a bit overwhelmed by Mr. Leary's reaction, and I began to wonder if my master plan may have actually been a huge mistake. I had never been to the principal's office before. With the exception of Mr. Leary, my teachers always seemed to like me, and I'd never been in any real trouble.

Mr. Leary had already called ahead, so by the time I got to the principal's office, they were expecting me.

Before I could explain myself, they sent me in to talk to the school psychologist. I guess that's mandatory when students destroy property. I was encouraged to share my feelings, so I explained the infinite detention loop and the detention-instigation plan designed to break the loop.

Eventually, the psychologist grew frustrated that she was unable to "connect" with me.

The principal said she was going to call my parents in so we could sort everything out. Thankfully, my dad worked too far away to make it in time. But my mom worked close by, and she was going to come in and get me after school.

I spent the rest of the day in Principal Kimbell's office until the final bell rang, and she sent me back to the classroom to gather my books. I picked up my homework assignments from Mrs. Rosario, but I decided to ask Billy for whatever homework Mr. Leary had assigned. I figured it would be a good idea to avoid Mr. Leary altogether. Unfortunately, he saw me and assumed I was trying to escape.

I can't say I was surprised Mr. Leary was still upset. That was the plan, after all. But I was caught offguard when he suddenly snatched my book bag away from me.

I don't know why he thought my book bag was full of toys, but there's a lot I don't understand about that guy. I think he would have slammed my bag on the floor, but Mrs. Rosario and all the other students were watching as they were getting ready to leave, so he reluctantly gave me my bag back.

As I walked back to the principal's office, I realized everyone was looking at me and pointing, whispering to each other. Then somebody grabbed my shoulder, and I thought I was about to get in a fight. I spun around to face my brother Dave… and I still thought I was about to get in a fight. He normally didn't like for me to try to hang around with him in school since it cramped his style, but today it was all different. Dave said word about the diploma incident had spread around the school, and everyone thought I was awesome. He proudly walked me the rest of the way to the principal's office as I received nods of approval and high fives from a lot of other students, even the bigger kids.

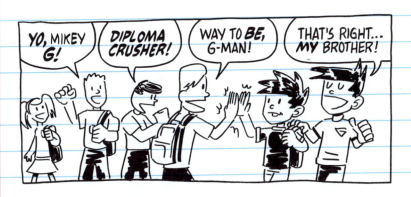

I felt like a new superhero who had just defeated a tyrannical supervillain!

Unfortunately, I had not yet defeated my foe, and the principal's office staff continued to behave as if the only villain in this scenario was me. ME!

At least they didn't keep bothering me. I finished all the homework assignments I had for the day, and then my mom finally showed up. Principal Kimbell called Mr. Leary in. This was going to be my last chance to explain the whole story.

It started out with my mom and Mr. Leary agreeing that I was a troublemaker and a liar. Eventually, they got on the topic of my recent time spent in detention.

It suddenly became clear to everyone that I wasn't lying about anything.

Rather than slow down to acknowledge my honesty, Mr. Leary shifted attention away from that awkward revelation and started the diploma talk. He said there was NO excuse for the destruction of his diploma. At last, I thought I finally had everyone on the same page, so I once again tried to explain my behavior was a desperate attempt to break the infinite detention loop.

My mom said she'd pay for a replacement diploma and the money would be coming directly out of my allowance.

I don't actually get an allowance, but I sensed this was not the appropriate time to sidebar for an allowance discussion. The offer only seemed to enrage Mr. Leary further.

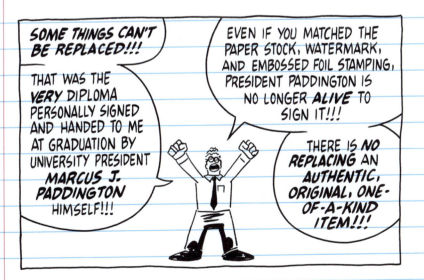

That was when I finally opened up my bag to reveal...

... Mr. Leary's diploma, intact and unscathed. My mom, Principal Kimbell, and the psychologist crowded around Mr. Leary in silent disbelief. Mr. Leary just stared at it, trying to make sense of how I had magically undone the damage, but too proud to ask. Maybe being smart is a superpower after all.

After examining it from all angles, Mr. Leary confirmed with Principal Kimbell that it was indeed his original, authentic diploma. He looked at me like he was going to say something, but then he just walked out of the room without saying another word.

Then I asked Principal Kimbell if I had to serve any more detentions or not. She sighed and just told me to go home — you know, like she was exasperated from the whole ordeal, and this was her dramatic way to end the day. I was not satisfied with her ambiguous response. For all I knew, Mr. Leary was already scheming to put me in another detention loop. So I had to ask again, because after everything I'd been through, I wasn't going to walk out of there without a straight answer.

On the way home, my mom kept asking me how I had

managed to pull off the diploma stunt, and I just kept telling her "magic" until she stopped asking. I didn't want to tell her I actually busted one of HER frames in class.

It took Dave only a few minutes to find an image of a diploma from Mr Leary's university on the Internet. He used his computer graphics skills to add Mr. Leary's name, and we printed it out on thick card stock paper.

Then we inserted it into the frame we had chosen from my

mom's collection. It may not have fooled anyone under close examination, but to the casual observer, it would easily pass for the real thing.

During recess, which I had to spend in Mr. Leary's classroom, I simply waited for his usual coffee run to the teachers' lounge.

In that brief, unsupervised window of time, I switched out Mr. Leary's diploma for the fake that Dave had created, concealing the real diploma in my book bag. Then I just waited through math class for the perfect moment to destroy the fake in front of everyone!

I DID it! I broke the infinite detention loop! I'm free and clear to go to Suntrooper tryouts! I'M GOING TO BE A SUNTROOPER!!! I'M FINALLY GOING TO BE A SUPERHERO!!!

TUESDAY

Today was day one of Suntrooper tryouts! However, because there was such a huge turnout, they decided to split up the boys and girls into different days. So only the girls go today, and boys go tomorrow. Jen Goodwell started talking trash as soon as we found out.

She always talks that way in an attempt to get a friendly rivalry going with us, but it backfires on her almost every time.

As excited as I was to put on a solar suit and start flying, I was actually glad that the girls were going first. I considered it a tactical advantage. I planned to attend the girls' tryouts as a spectator to learn as much as I could about what was in store for us the next day.

I planned to study the most subtle detail of every challenge.

I planned to assimilate all successful strategies.

This was my big chance to become a superhero, and I wanted all odds in my favor. I was determined to be the most prepared candidate of the bunch!

But when the time came, there was no real opportunity for me to gain any special insights or tactical advantage...

It turned out Suntrooper tryouts are nothing more than a round of the same physical fitness testing we did every year in gym class. No solar suits, no flying, no blasting. No awesome.

But the bright side is I usually do really well in those tests. Actually, without Billy or Sunny in the mix, it's basically going to be a competition between Curtis and me to see who's the best in our class. While it's true that Eddie Delta is a great athlete, he's not quite as big and strong as the rest of us. He excels more in the realm of the hand-eye coordination

involved with dribbling and shooting baskets, rather than
the brute strength and speed they measure in these fitness
tests. But I'm sure we'll all do well enough to pass tryouts,
and we can all become Suntroopers together!

A squadron of Suntroopers departs for a space mission.

WEDNESDAY

Today was the boys' turn for Suntrooper tryouts. And since everyone in the school thought I was so cool after the diploma incident, I figured it would be okay to hang out with my brother and his friends.

Turns out I was wrong about that. Meanwhile, Tony Carboni somehow got it in his head that he was the best.

At first I couldn't understand Tony's confidence, since Curtis and I were the strongest and fastest kids in our class. Tony wasn't even close to our level. Then it became clear.

Tony was still under the impression we were going to be wearing solar suits, and he figured his limited experience with Sunny's suit in gym class gave him an advantage.

The Suntrooper's obvious sarcasm failed to register with Tony, and we couldn't think of any reason to set him straight.

Curtis and I ended up doing our push-ups at the same time, side by side. I could see him next to me in my peripheral vision. My plan was to match him push-up for push-up so I could hang on just long enough to do at least one more repetition than he did. But Curtis was trying to outdo me with the exact same strategy.

We both reached failure after fifty-one push-ups. We stood up, our arms exhausted and our egos expanded, for we were certain we probably set some sort of record for our class and possibly the whole school. However...

Eddie Delta did a HUNDRED push-ups! He shattered the class AND school record! We couldn't believe it! And he wasn't even tired. I think he just stopped out of boredom, or he just didn't want to hold up tryouts from progressing.

It was awesome, but I was puzzled. We never considered Eddie to be that strong because he's somewhat smaller than us. Then the same thing happened with pull-ups. Curtis and I each did twelve pull-ups, which I would ordinarily have felt proud of, but Eddie went to thirty, again stopping before he was actually tired.

Curtis was right. Something else is going on with Eddie. His muscle strength and endurance is off the charts. I was thinking maybe he eats a really good breakfast.

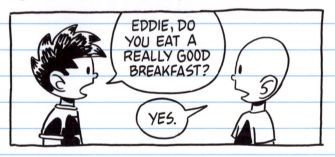

I KNEW IT!

Next we performed the agility test, which is a side-to-side shuffle back and forth across three lines.

The goal is to cross as many lines as possible in thirty seconds. This time, I beat Curtis with a score of thirty-one, while he only got a twenty-eight. I was feeling good about that until I realized WHY I beat him.

Curtis was hoping to get a do-over, but the Suntroopers wouldn't let him.

YOUR SCORE IS ALREADY WELL WITHIN THE QUALIFYING RANGE.

YOU DON'T HAVE TO TAKE THIS SO SERIOUSLY. IT'S NOT THE OLYMPICS.

Then Eddie scored a FIFTY-NINE! The Suntroopers balked at this, and they made him go again.

The Suntroopers couldn't believe Eddie's quickness, and they didn't want to record a false high score. This time, everyone was watching to verify Eddie's performance.

We thought it was unfair to make him go again right away without adequate rest, but it didn't matter. He didn't seem to slow down when he changed direction the way the rest of us do. He was a human blur of speed and colors.

We still had to run a couple races, but there was no way
Curtis would be able to run in his busted shoe.

When the Suntrooper said earlier that Curtis was in
qualifying range, he meant in each event SO FAR. Curtis (and
everyone) still had to qualify in the races for acceptance
into Suntrooper basic training. The races were split into
several waves because there were too many kids to run all
at once. So I just let Curtis wear my sneakers, and we ran in
different waves. Tony thought I was being foolish.

Tony just doesn't get it. If I beat somebody, I don't want
it to be because of some fluke mistake. That wouldn't
be a true victory, and it would be nothing to be proud of.
Plus, I wanted Curtis to do well so we could all become
Suntroopers together. Neither of us turned out to be the
fastest, anyway. Guess who easily recorded the best time
in both the hundred-meter dash and the mile run? Even my
brother was impressed.

I was still wondering how Eddie had managed to surprise
everyone. We do these tests once a year in gym class, and I

didn't remember him ever making such a big impact before, so I asked him about it.

What are the chances of that?

Anyway, everybody qualified in the physical fitness portion of the Suntrooper tryouts, even Tony. Tomorrow, we'll be doing the academic testing. Sunny said it's all multiple choice and way easier than anything we've ever done in school. So it looks like nothing can stop me from qualifying for Suntrooper training now, and I'm that much closer to becoming a Suntrooper superhero!

THURSDAY

I was disqualified from Suntrooper tryouts.

All I had to do was pass the SUPER EASY multiple choice exam, and I would have been in! But I got busted for cheating! CHEATING!!!

WHY would I cheat? I knew EVERYTHING on that test! Probably the EASIEST test of ALL TIME!

Tony Carboni was copying off my paper! I didn't know! I wasn't paying attention to HIM. I was paying attention to the TEST!

But one of the Suntroopers caught him, and he said that I was a willing accomplice.

They removed us from the testing area and made us wait in the teachers' lounge. Suddenly, Tony was all buddy-buddy with me and talking like we were equally responsible for this unfortunate predicament HE put us in.

Naturally, Tony didn't understand I was being sarcastic. Unfortunately, neither did the Suntrooper who was watching us. He took my comment literally, as though I really did consider Tony to be a cool guy. From there, the Suntrooper leapt to the conclusion that I was trying to help Tony cheat because I so desperately desired Tony's friendship and approval. And he said all of this right in front of Tony, reinforcing Tony's already enormous ego.

That was when Mr. Leary walked in to get some coffee. He sipped his coffee and treated himself to the entertaining self-esteem lecture. After he'd thoroughly enjoyed himself...

It was a laugh that told me he'd pieced together the whole situation. He wasn't laughing at me for getting caught cheating. He knew I wasn't a cheater, and he knew I didn't like Tony. He was laughing because he knew I was unjustifiably being punished, and he knew my opportunity to be a Suntrooper and a superhero had just been wasted. He walked out delighted.

We remained in the teachers' lounge while the testing continued in the gym. Different Suntroopers were constantly coming and going during that time, getting coffee or water and chatting with each other. We couldn't help overhearing their conversations. It's not like they were trying to keep secrets from us, and there was literally nothing else for us to do but sit and listen.

Because of this, we wound up hearing about some big news with the bioscans. Suntroopers have all kinds of scanning equipment built into their gloves.

While everyone was seated taking exams, the Suntroopers took bioscans of each student. It's kind of like a blood test but without having to take any blood. They can read our blood type, DNA, and other genetic information noninvasively.

So the big news was...

THAT COLOR-CHANGER KID WHO BROKE ALL THOSE RECORDS YESTERDAY IS HALF ELF!

WELL, *THAT* EXPLAINS A LOT!

Eddie Delta became the focus of every Suntrooper conversation in the teachers' lounge for the rest of the day. Elves come in all different colors, but with only partial elf DNA, Eddie Delta's color genes never stabilized. Elves aren't generally as strong as humans, but they are significantly quicker on their feet. In Eddie's case, his elf quickness multiplied his human muscle endurance, so he's much stronger than an average elf OR human.

Just when I thought Eddie Delta couldn't be any cooler!

When I got home later, I told my brother Dave all about it, but he didn't seem very impressed. It was as if he was participating in a completely different conversation.

HA HA, I'M GOING TO BE A SUNTROOPER, AND YOU'RE NOT!

The Suntrooper tryouts results were posted this morning on a wall just inside the school lobby. Unfortunately, this caused a huge crowd to form as everyone struggled to see if they passed the tryouts.

The crowding became dangerous, so Sunny had to step in and take control of the situation.

I guess that was the most efficient way to stop everyone from climbing all over each other and suffocating. They never

should have posted that list in the lobby to begin with.
They could have just mentioned everybody qualified during
the morning school announcements. And maybe Sunny didn't
actually need to blurt out the names of the two disqualified
students who were well aware of their fate already, but
I understand he didn't have time to think it through.
Unfortunately for me, that meant dealing with a continuous
stream of this...

This was not my favorite day of school.
Science class was just more of the same.

Tony was having an equally rough day, which caused him to
gravitate to me for solidarity during recess.

I'm sure you'll be SHOCKED to know what happened next.

Can you even believe that Tony would completely turn on me and lie? I told you it would be shocking. That's when Eddie Delta stepped in to defend me.

Tony's accusation kind of caught everyone by surprise, INCLUDING Eddie. But that didn't stop Tony. It just encouraged him to continue.

This seemed like a BIG secret — a PRIVATE secret that Eddie was not even aware of. I didn't think Eddie was going to want to have to deal with everyone asking him about elves when he didn't even know about it himself, so my instinct was to discredit Tony immediately. I was on the spot! I needed to think fast and talk even faster. I racked my brain for the best way to phrase it, and somehow, under pressure, I managed to come up with the perfect response to Tony's question.

Tony was stunned. There was no recovering from the verbal onslaught I had just unleashed upon him.

Determined to avoid continuous teasing for his cheating, Tony gave up on Eddie and turned his attack to an easier target — Curtis.

Curtis has been wearing flip-flops to school ever since his sneaker fell apart. He knew he was inviting the chants. Like me, he was trying to keep the focus off of the elf talk.

Unlike me, he did not care at all about getting teased. Curtis actually THRIVED on getting the crowd riled up.

Meanwhile, with the playground's attention now focused entirely on Curtis, the rest of us slipped away. I finally had a chance to talk to Eddie privately. He was looking for answers.

This was an awkward position to be in, and I felt like this highly sensitive topic needed to be discussed delicately. I racked my brain for the best way to phrase it, and somehow, under pressure, I managed to come up with the perfect response to Eddie's question.

To experience such a powerful revelation about one's own origin is not the easiest thing to face. Eddie had to question everything he knew about himself. Who WAS he? Where did he COME from? Would it be too much for Eddie Delta to handle?

I think it was not too much for Eddie Delta to handle.

SATURDAY

This weekend started out relatively normal.

Something is always my fault. The thing that's my fault this time is that my dad won't let Dave enroll in Suntrooper basic training.

Yup. Entirely MY fault.

Then Eddie Delta came by. At first I thought he was coming over to hang out and play, but today his mom was with him. She wanted to discuss Eddie's bioscan. I told her what the Suntroopers said in the teachers' lounge about Eddie being half elf.

Eddie's mom asked Dave and me to promise not to tell anybody else.

Dave asked why we can't tell anybody, but my dad said that was a rude question to ask. But Eddie's mom answered anyway and said she was just worried about Eddie being teased at school. I guess she doesn't realize everyone thinks Eddie is totally cool and that elves are also totally cool. But if she wants us to keep it a secret, we will.

Eddie's mom asked me who else knew. I told her how Tony Carboni was also in the teachers' lounge, and how he was the one who let the secret loose during recess. Unfortunately, there's no way to tell how many kids believed him or would remember or even care. There was also a good chance that Tony would bring it up again and again and again... ESPECIALLY if you asked him NOT to.

Sometimes it can be awkward to have somebody walk in while you're saying unflattering things about them. Other times, it can be awesome.

Tony's dad was with him, and he was really angry.

Mr. Carboni aggressively approached my dad.

The Suntroopers sent all the qualifying kids home with permission forms to have their parents sign in order to officially enroll in the Junior Suntrooper training program.

While Dave went to get the forms, Mr. Carboni proceeded to give my dad a piece of his mind. I had never heard anybody talk to my dad that way before, and I was absolutely puzzled by how calm my dad remained. Mr. Carboni told my dad he would not stand for the way I had ruined Tony's chance of becoming a Suntrooper. He stepped closer and closer while telling my dad to be ashamed of raising a lying cheater, and that I needed a lesson in personal responsibility.

Mr. Carboni insisted my dad "do something about this or else," as he got right up in my dad's face and thumped his finger on my dad's chest.

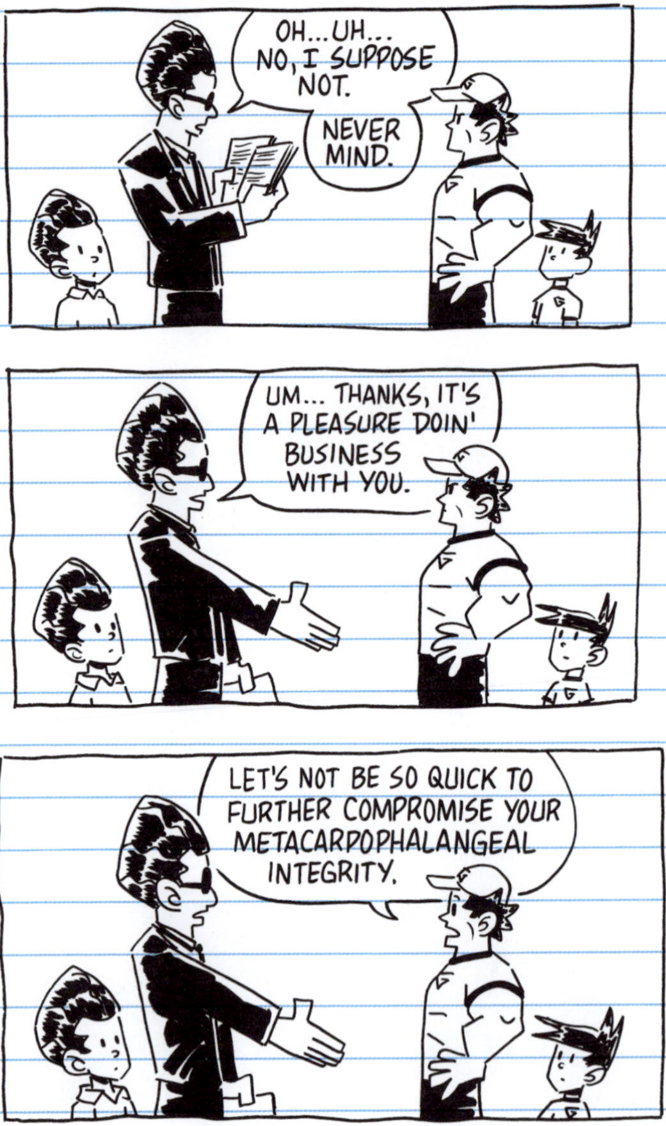
OH...UH... NO, I SUPPOSE NOT.
NEVER MIND.
UM... THANKS, IT'S A PLEASURE DOIN' BUSINESS WITH YOU.
LET'S NOT BE SO QUICK TO FURTHER COMPROMISE YOUR METACARPOPHALANGEAL INTEGRITY.

The problem with the forms is that by signing them, parents turn legal custody of their kids over to the Suntroopers, effectively giving their kids away to the Suntrooper Space Force to do whatever they want, whenever they want.

But Dave would prefer to think it's MY fault my dad won't let him enroll.

I wish my dad would sign the forms so the Suntroopers could send Dave to Jupiter.

SUNDAY

There was even MORE big Suntrooper news TODAY! The
Suntrooper Space Force held a major press conference to
announce the Color Guardians are LEAVING the Color Queen
to become Suntroopers! I guess it's like they are graduating
and moving on to the big leagues.

I always thought that the Color Guardians had powers
very similar to the Suntroopers', so I'm not surprised to
learn there is some sort of association between the two
organizations. I guess the Color Guardians are sort of an
unofficial farm team for the Suntrooper Space Force.

My dad says the timing is a strategic publicity stunt designed to influence parents. The Suntroopers are presenting the advancement of the Color Guardians as a wise and glamorous path to take, just as parents all over the city are deciding whether or not to allow their own children to enroll.

MONDAY

Pretty much everybody was bummed out at school today because everyone's parents refused to let them enroll in the Junior Suntrooper training program. It was the main topic of conversation during homeroom.

Some kids wondered why Sunny's parents were okay with him being a Suntrooper, but most were polite enough not to say anything about it.

Sunny's parents are actually both retired Suntroopers and still work for the Suntrooper Space Force, so they are given a lot more control over Sunny than an ordinary civilian parent would have, and they're a lot more comfortable with the Suntrooper program as a whole.

And then things took a bad turn...

This was not good. We were hoping Tony would just forget about the elf thing completely, but here he was, already raising the issue again.

What?

After Eddie and his mom left my house this weekend, they went to go visit Sunny. They knew they could never trust Tony, so they came up with a simple plan to fool him by discrediting Eddie's previous bioscan.

The bigger news of the day was Curtis's new sneakers. Curtis finally had a chance to go shoe shopping over the weekend. While everyone else was wallowing away in disappointment over not getting Suntrooper powers, Curtis was out getting super-speed powers from a pair of the fastest sneakers in the world!

His shoes are MAGIC. They have wings that flare out from the ankles, and they seem to kick off sparks of light. Not fire sparks, but more like glowing magic sparks.

And the shoes give him super speed, so Curtis is basically like Racing Stripe now. Racing Stripe is another one of my favorite superheroes. He's our city's most famous super speedster, always "fighting crime in the nick of time," as they say in the news.

City speedster Racing Stripe slows down just long enough to smile for the camera.

Racing Stripe doesn't wear magic shoes though. He says he gets his powers from "extreme meditative focus."

Not surprisingly, Tony was the first one to ask...

Everyone wanted to try them on during recess, but nobody chased Curtis the way they had chased Billy and Sunny around. Curtis was way too fast to be chased. Everyone just watched him circle the playground and the soccer fields, a human blur followed by a trail of sparks.

I think "Sparky" is going to catch on better than "Flip-Flop" did. And eventually, he actually DID let ONE person try his shoes.

Tony did not get to go next.

I couldn't believe it! I FINALLY got to experience having a superpower! Sparky told me to run only two laps around the playground... but I just couldn't stop! The shoes moved me faster than I expected them to. It was exhilarating!

There was an odd time distortion, a strange sensation where after a certain point, it stopped feeling like I was moving faster, but everything else around me seemed like it slowed down. I can't help wondering if that's somehow related to the "meditative focus" that Racing Stripe talks about.

Before I even realized it, I had run thirty laps around the playground. Finally, I stopped running and took off the shoes.

He knew?

Sparky said the same thing had happened to him the first time he took the shoes off. He told me to put the shoes back on. Doing so instantly relieved my leg pain, but he warned me not to run any more until my body had a chance to recover.

Actually, Sparky told me he got them at Manny's Shoe Store on Blake Street from a salesman named Gregory. We switched shoes back at the end of the day (my legs were still a little sore, but feeling a lot better by then), and I went home. I begged my mom to take me to Manny's Shoe Store. I suddenly had another opportunity for superpowers within reach, and I didn't want to lose it! We HAD to get there before word spread and they sold out!

Dave wanted to come along because he was guaranteed to benefit no matter how the situation turned out. Either there WOULD be magic shoes...

... or there WOULDN'T be.

Unfortunately for me, it was the "told you so" scenario. We didn't see any magic shoes on the shelf, so I tried describing the shoes to the salespeople. They did not seem to be taking me seriously.

I asked if Gregory was working. They all said they had never heard of any Gregory. Dave was enjoying every second of my frustration. Then suddenly, this guy comes strolling out of the back room.

I was confused. They literally JUST told me they had NEVER heard of the guy.

Now that I was dealing with Gregory, it was a whole different ball game.

He said they were a one-of-a-kind item. I was beginning to think this guy was just humoring us to get us out of the store, and Sparky had made the whole thing up in order to keep the truth a secret. Dave continued to laugh as we walked out, when Gregory added one last thing...

I had never mentioned Sparky by name or that I had worn his shoes. That kind of freaked us out. Dave stopped teasing me after that.

Now I can't stop wondering — where did those magic shoes ORIGINALLY came from, BEFORE they ended up in that shoe store? Maybe they came from another planet...

Maybe they were in some sort of science experiment...

Or maybe the shoes were in some kind of technology accident...

Maybe I should start looking for superpowers on top-secret Japanese websites.

TUESDAY

Today, Sparky came to school with a full superhero costume to go along with the shoes and the windshield visor. The design of the symbol on his chest is like a burst of energy that represents a spark.

But Sparky was not the only one to show up in a new costume today.

Jen, Sheila, and Grace are now members of the all-new Color Guardians! Color Queen went undercover to all the Suntrooper tryouts to scope out talent for a new team.

Color Queen presents her new team of Color Guardians.

Jen is the new Red Girl, Sheila is the new Green Girl, and Grace is the new Blue Girl. The other four new Guardians go to different schools. They have fancy princess names, but they are hard to remember.

I'm sure we'll remember the princess names eventually. And I'm sure we'll continue to call Jen "Red Girl" long after that... at least as long as it continues to annoy her. I don't see what the big deal is. They DO go through the trouble of dressing up in specific colors, after all. The other girls don't seem to mind so much.

Inevitably, other kids wanted to try out their suits.

It's the same deal as Sunny's solar suit. The girls aren't allowed to let anyone else wear their Guardian suits.

It was cool watching them all flying around in superhero costumes during recess. And I'm glad that they all get to have powers, but I have to admit I'm starting to feel bummed out.

It's hard to stay excited for everyone else when deep down, I feel like I'm missing out on all the superhero fun. I've wanted superpowers forever, and every time I turn around, somebody else is getting superpowers instead. And getting superpowers is so rare and random, the odds of me ALSO getting powers are now astronomically against me.

I don't have elf DNA, my dad won't ever let me be a Suntrooper, there are no more magic shoes available, and the Color Guardians are girls only.

Maybe I can still figure out how to build a pair of wings like Billy's. I got so distracted with other stuff, I never did get around to asking him how he built them. I need to see his designs.

WEDNESDAY

Unbelievable! Guess who showed up in costume today? TONY!
He had a harness with wings like Billy Demon's, winged shoes
like Sparky's, and even a body suit that changes colors to
mimic Eddie Delta's camouflage effects! It's like the universe
has decided very specifically to play a practical joke at
my expense.

Are you KIDDING me? There's REALLY a Japanese website
where you can order superhero gear?!!!

Tony's wings actually seemed more high-tech than Billy's.
They looked a lot like Technohawk's wings.

Technohawk will not rest until he has justice.

Other kids were eager to try out Tony's new equipment.

At recess, we were treated to a full display of Tony's new super skills. He focused on the wings first. He was having a lot of trouble getting those to work properly, so he spent a lot of time asking Billy for tips.

Tony couldn't get the wing flapping down properly, but Billy said it took him a lot of practice when he first got his own wings. I guess it must be like learning to ride a bike. Most people can't do it the first time they try, but once you get the hang of it, it becomes natural. Billy suggested Tony start with the basics of gliding. I have to admit I found it annoying that Billy would bother to help Tony out at all.

With a good running start, Tony was able to glide for some considerable distance, but nothing that really took him higher than ground level. I had a strange feeling of déjà vu watching him. I've had dreams where I was doing exactly what he was doing — intermittently gliding at ground level while running.

Speaking of Tony's running start, that was when I noticed his sneakers did absolutely nothing to enhance his speed. They were just sneakers that had cool-looking wings on them, but they were not magic at all. I found that revelation somewhat satisfying.

After some more running and gliding, Tony began overheating. That color-changing outfit he was wearing was like a thermal bodysuit — not the most comfortable choice for running around in warm weather.

EDDIE, HOW CAN YOU STAND THE **HEAT** IN ONE OF THESE COLOR-CHANGING SUITS?

I DRINK A LOT OF WATER.

IT'S ALL ABOUT HYDRATION.

I don't know how Tony missed the obvious fact that his color suit is not actually similar to anything Eddie has ever worn, but if Tony has reverted to believing that Eddie's powers come from a gadget or a gimmick instead of elf DNA, that's a good thing.

As Tony resumed his gliding, I was fully steeped in jealousy. Maybe it was the déjà vu feeling from my dreams, but I couldn't help feeling like I deserved to be the one flying, not TONY CARBONI of all people! I want wings of my OWN.

I began asking Billy lots of questions about his wings. I noticed that his and Tony's wings were similar, but not exactly the same. Billy said there are a lot of different variations on the basic design, but as he had mentioned before, they're really expensive to buy or even to build on your own. I think he was anticipating I might ask him again if I could try his wings, so he started going over the reasons why he couldn't let anybody wear them again.

Suddenly, my jealousy subsided, but I'm still going to have to do some research into buying or building my own pair of wings. I MUST FLY!

THURSDAY

I can't believe what Billy did in science class today!

Mr. Leary assigned us a research paper and said it could be on a science-related topic of our choice. Billy asked if he could do his paper on the chemistry of combustible candy, explaining when you combine cinnamon-hot fireball candy with crackling fizzy pops candy in your mouth, it creates an explosion. Everyone has heard of this phenomenon. Allegedly, Phillip Michael Lucas, the child actor who portrayed Curly Greene on the old TV sitcom "Greene House," actually died from doing this.

Billy pulled out a fireball and a pack of fizzy pops and walked up to the front of the classroom.

At this point, I couldn't help thinking that if it had been ME up there, Mr. Leary would have already told me to sit down and possibly assigned me a detention. But he let Billy continue, maybe because Billy is Billy, and everybody likes Billy. Or maybe Mr. Leary wanted to see what would happen just as much as the rest of us.

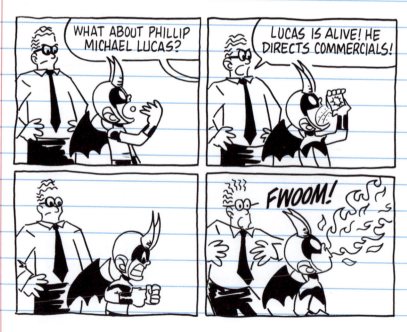

The look on Mr. Leary's face was priceless... not that we didn't all have the same look of shock. The urban myth was TRUE! Mr. Leary told Billy to sit down and "never ever ever ever ever pull a stunt like that in his classroom or anywhere else ever again." He said it was dangerous to Billy and to every student and teacher in the school. For once, I found myself in full agreement with Mr. Leary. I wasn't eager to see one of my best friends' head explode.

At first I couldn't believe Billy didn't earn an instant detention. But then I considered how his detention letter would sound to his mom.

Mr. Leary would probably prefer there to be no written record of Billy's pyrotechnic demonstration in his classroom.

So it looks like Billy will have to choose a different topic for his research paper. Mr. Leary said we would be visiting the library for class tomorrow to work on our research, so we would have the rest of the day and night to pick a topic. I've already decided I'll be researching winged suits. I might even be able to get my parents to buy wing-building materials if I can convince them it's for a school project!

FRIDAY

Today, we went to the library for science class to start our research projects. Right away, I found a book with some diagrams and drawings of different types of glider wings.

They didn't look like the heavily armored wings that Cyber Demon and Technohawk use. They were more similar to the sleeker lightweight design of Billy's wings. But there were also sketches of bird wings.

That's when I realized the basic structure of Billy's wings were probably the same as the structure of the feathered wings of superheroes like Emerald Eagle and Blue Jason. In fact, the feathers actually seem to reduce wind resistance!

Emerald Eagle soars high over the city rooftops.

Blue Jason streaks across the sky to answer the call for justice.

I was pretty excited that my research was already going so well. I was definitely on my way to building a superhero suit AND turning it into my research report! Mr. Leary wandered over to see what I was doing.

We now have SEVEN superheroes in our class with real superheroes who wear superhero costumes, and yet he still chooses to give ME a hard time about the whole superhero thing. At that point, I knew I had no chance of getting his approval for my research topic.

What?

I don't know how he was missing the plain fact that I was looking at winged superhero suits, but I decided it would be best to just roll with it.

I found some more books about aeronautics and checked them out of the library.

As soon as I got home from school, I went straight to work on my report. I wanted to get it out of the way as quickly as possible so I could use the rest of the weekend to work on building some wings. Plus, I'm going to go hang out with the guys at the park tomorrow, and I can't enjoy myself if I know I have a big homework assignment like a report hanging over my head. I'm always intimidated by the idea of writing reports, and I thought it was going to be really difficult. Dave scoffed.

Later on, while I was working on the report, there was a major breaking-news story — Captain Thunderman had defeated Mister Mental!!!

It started with Mister Mental doing some sort of street performance in the park.

Street performers generally put on shows in public to attract attention from the masses of people that happen to be around, and then they take donations after they are done performing. I saw these acrobat guys one time doing all kinds of crazy jumping and tumbling and balancing tricks. They were AMAZING, and every person in the crowd gave them like a dollar or five dollars or whatever. So I guess Mister Mental was trying to put on a show like that, but all he ended up doing were some jumping jacks.

Of course, Mister Mental was psychically forcing people to "donate" every last dollar they may have had on them with his mental mind-control powers. Word of his scam spread, and eventually it caught Captain Thunderman's attention, who flew in to put a stop to it.

The crowd began to surround Captain Thunderman, as Mister Mental commanded them to swarm. It was his usual tactic of distraction and escape. But Captain Thunderman grabbed

him and flew him up into the sky before any of the people
could interfere or get hurt.

Captain Thunderman flew as high and far as he could to keep
Mister Mental out of range of any other innocent people
he might be able to control. Mister Mental grew desperate
and managed to get an arm loose enough to knock Captain
Thunderman's helmet off.

This made Captain Thunderman vulnerable to a psychic attack!

Mister Mental was so desperate to escape, he forgot where he was!

But it was too late. Captain Thunderman wasn't able to get there in time.

The Lava Lords Volcano Energy Corporation immediately initiated an emergency extraction protocol, but there's really not much you can do for a guy who just fell into a reservoir of molten lava. Mister Mental is dead!

Then angry guys argued about it all over the news for the rest of the night.

At least in THIS house, everyone is celebrating — even my dad — so I decided to put my project on hold. It's almost done, and I'm pretty sure I can finish it tomorrow morning.

SATURDAY

While I was finishing up the rest of my aeronautics report this morning, I noticed that one of the books I brought home from the library was not actually about airplanes or rockets or any science of flying machines. It was about superheroes! Titled "How to Fly," it specifically explains the different methods by which superheroes are able to fly! I finished my report, but instead of building wings as previously planned, reading "How to Fly" instantly became my immediate priority.

I figured I should be up high if I was going to start flying, so I climbed up on the roof with "How to Fly" and began reading.

I felt like an idiot. The whole first chapter was about how jumping off roofs or cliffs or out of trees is stupid and dangerous. It only results in injury or death. There is no advantage to starting out from high places.

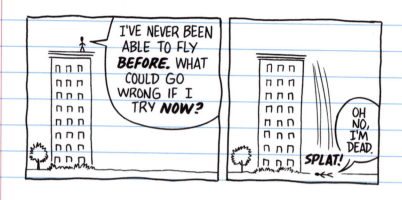

Think about it — superheroes take off from ground level all the time. That's how beginners ought to start as well.

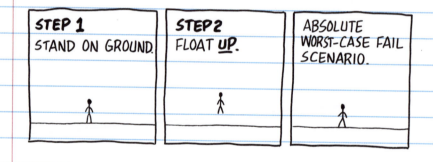

I went back inside the house and began reading about the metaphysics involved with supernatural flight. For example, dressing properly is an important aspect I never thoroughly considered before. I thought a superhero costume was just for looking cool, but it also helps send a subliminal signal to the surrounding environment and universe that you can defy certain scientific principles. Maybe that scientific defiance is one of the reasons Mr. Leary doesn't like superheroes.

I quickly assembled my own costume. I put on a shirt with a bigger G (we have a lot of different G-shirts) and a pair of sweatpants, and I put some wristbands on my wrists and ankles. But a cape is considered the most important part of the costume in terms of gravity defiance, so I grabbed a random cape from our box of Halloween costumes.

I began my levitation meditation when Dave happened by. Completely unfamiliar with what I was doing, his natural impulse was to criticize me.

Dave was already gone before I could show him the part about capes in the book, but that was when I noticed an extra detail I had previously missed.

MAGIC CAPES WORK BEST.

That made a lot of sense. OF COURSE magic would be helpful in supernaturally defying science! That's how Sparky's shoes work! It's so obvious, I can't believe I didn't think of it myself! I immediately thought of our magic blanket. I never believed it was actually magical before, but I figured it couldn't hurt to give it a shot. When I tried the levitation technique with the magic blanket...

.... something just clicked. I felt a surge of power in my body, and suddenly I was floating right there in the hallway!!! It felt as natural as walking! The blanket was too big to be manageable, so I cut a piece from it that would be perfect cape size. I couldn't wait to fly over to the park to show the guys my new powers!

I was really doing it! My greatest fantasy had come true!

It was the single greatest moment I'd ever experienced!

FINALLY, after ALL THIS TIME...

... after watching all my friends get superpowers one by one...

... after all my own failed attempts...

I FINALLY had superpowers of my OWN! I was FLYING!!!

It was everything I'd ever wanted! For once in my life, everything was absolutely perfect!

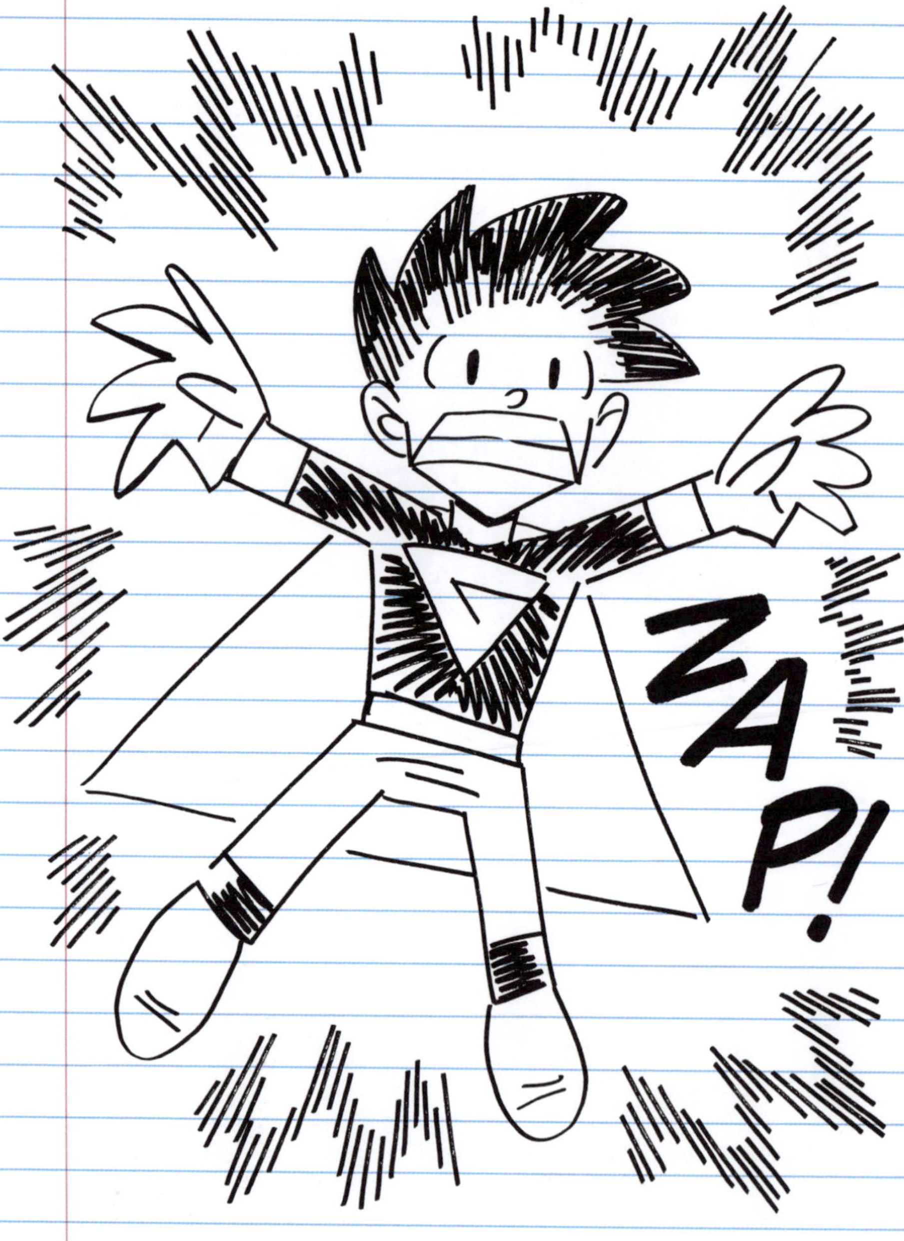
ZAP!

Just my luck. I can't even enjoy superpowers for two minutes without someone ruining it. Somebody blasted me right out of the sky, and I crash-landed in the park. Fortunately, although the wind was knocked out of me and I felt banged up, I was basically unharmed. The magic of the cape protected me from suffering any real injury. I had defied science yet again. I'm sure Mr. Leary would have disapproved yet again.

Billy, Sunny, Sparky, and Eddie were all there to help me up when I finally got a look at my attacker. It was some bully dressed up like Captain Thunderman with a small robot army.

The bully turned out to be Captain Thunderman's son, Kid Thunder! Apparently, he decided that nobody but him should be allowed to fly around, and he'd been blasting everybody who dared to fly in "his" sky.

I didn't even know Captain Thunderman HAD a son, but I would have expected him to be a GOOD guy. His behavior made no logical sense.

I REALLY wanted to fight back and smash his dumb face in! EVERYONE wanted to smash Kid Thunder's dumb face in. But NOBODY wanted to risk the ultimate consequence of facing Capain Thunderman in a fight. Unfortunately, it seemed the best way to handle the situation was to just avoid Kid Thunder and hope he left us alone.

So after I left the house, Dave figured out how I used the magic blanket to get superpowers. He took some of the leftover magic blanket material and tied it around his waist as a belt, which granted him instant superpowers exactly like mine — flight, enhanced strength, and invulnerability. He flew to the park and ran into Kid Thunder the same as I did, but he was able to resist Kid Thunder's attack. Like me, Dave didn't realize Kid Thunder was Captain Thunderman's son, and he didn't hesitate to fight back.

Everyone in the park was cheering. They began chanting "G-MAN! G-MAN! G-MAN!" which SOUNDED good, but they were cheering for Dave, who also put a costume together with the family G on it. He was quick to correct everyone.

THAT DWEEB IS G-MAN. I'M *GREAT* MAN!

He always did say G-Man was a dumb nickname and the G should stand for something besides "G." So after Dave made it a point to punctuate his victory over Kid Thunder by publicly humiliating me, I didn't feel like sticking around to participate in the celebration.

The guys accompanied me back to my house, and that's when Captain Thunderman showed up with Kid Thunder looking for payback. CAPTAIN THUNDERMAN. At MY house. Due to the confusion created from Dave and me both wearing the letter G on our chests and the "G-Man" chants, Kid Thunder incorrectly identified ME as the guy who had beat him up! This was NOT how I had ever dreamed of meeting Captain Thunderman.

Could this day possibly get any more surreal?

The day got about eight hundred percent more surreal. Mister Mental was back from the dead and looking for revenge! Ordinarily that would be terrible, but in that moment, it actually SAVED me from a major beatdown!

Mister Mental was almost unrecognizable except for the energy brain on top of his head. I guess he must have fallen into the volcano like this...

So every part of him that was submerged had to be replaced by robotic cyborg parts! He said the Lava Lords had rescued him and rebuilt him. I don't know why anybody in their right mind would have done that...

... but I didn't have any time to think about that while there was a superhero battle unfolding in the front yard.

With Captain Thunderman momentarily incapacitated, Mister Mental turned his rage toward us, and WE were left to fight Mister Mental on our own! Fortunately, he didn't seem to be using his mind-control powers. Maybe he lost them as a result of being dropped in the volcano, or maybe he had to use all his mental concentration to make his new body work.

Whatever the case, we had to fight him. Sparky used his super speed to grab his cannon away. Billy Demon attacked him with his fire-breathing trick, and Sunny hit him with solar blasts to keep him off balance.

Then Eddie Delta distracted him while I snuck up behind him and pried his energy brain dome off his head.

His body collapsed and the fight was over, just as Captain Thunderman was recovering.

Okay, I didn't actually say that to him, but I WOULD have if I hadn't been surprised by the voice of Mister Mental coming from his energy brain making more threats! Startled, I dropped the dome on the ground, at which point my dad showed up and ran over it with the lawn mower. There will be no rebuilding Mister Mental this time.

With Mister Mental defeated and everyone calmed down, Dave
showed up with one of Kid Thunder's robots. He played some
of the robot's recorded footage that proved Kid Thunder
attacked me and several other kids. Captain Thunderman
made Kid Thunder apologize.

So now Dave's playing video games over at Thunder Tower
with his new best friend. What a great team THEY'LL make.

Things got off to a rocky start, but I think it turned out
to be a great first day of being a superhero! My friends

and I had our first ever super team-up, we defeated the biggest villain in the city, and we became friends with Captain Thunderman after a brief misunderstanding. It doesn't get any more classic than that!

MONDAY

I was excited to return to school today to show off my new superpowers, but everyone was already preoccupied with discussing the much bigger news of the day.

Kid Thunder just became the newest kid in our school. I guess he never had any friends before, and Captain Thunderman thought it would be good for him to hang out with my brother more often, so he arranged for Kid Thunder to transfer in. They're in all the same classes together.

So Kid Thunder, the son of the greatest and most famous superhero of all time, was all anyone could talk about.

I was jealous. It wasn't just that the new super celebrity was getting more attention than I was...

He was getting attention that should have belonged to ME AND THE GUYS!

You see, my dad told Captain Thunderman not to tell the news media that the guys and I were responsible for stopping Mister Mental. My dad is afraid Mister Mental's allies might come by looking for revenge or something, and he doesn't want to attract that kind of attention. So all the news reports credited Kid Thunder for helping Captain Thunderman defeat cyborg Mister Mental. And he wasn't even polite or gracious about all the attention he was getting!

The undue praise for Kid Thunder was driving me up the wall, and I couldn't even say anything about it! Even if my dad didn't tell me to keep my mouth shut, I knew things would have just gone like this anyway...

Making it even worse, they actually called a special morning assembly specifically to welcome Kid Thunder to our school and present him with a medal of valor!

Then Kid Thunder said a few words to the school.

...IT SICKENS ME.

BECAUSE I KNOW I DON'T DESERVE IT.
DEFEATING MISTER MENTAL IS A NOTEWORTHY ACCOMPLISHMENT, BUT I HAD NOTHING TO DO WITH IT.
I WATCHED FROM THE SIDELINES WHILE THE REAL HEROES STEPPED UP AND GOT THE JOB DONE.

I CAN'T ACCEPT THIS MEDAL.

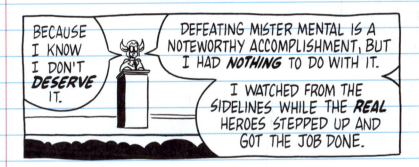

I was NOT expecting THAT. None of us were.

It felt pretty great.

The rest of the day shaped up rather nicely after that.

My brother even let me hang out with him and Kid Thunder during recess. Mrs. Rosario took pictures.

Of course Tony wanted to try my cape, but I wouldn't let him.

Then he moved on to Kid Thunder.

Even science class went incredibly well. I got an A+ on my aeronautics report, which was surprising because Mr. Leary didn't seem to be at all pleased while I was reading it in front of the classroom.

At the end of the day, Mrs. Rosario printed out photos and gave us each a copy.

I can't wait for our next adventure!

MORE TO EXPLORE!

AH, LEONARDO DA VINCI! EXCELLENT!
-?

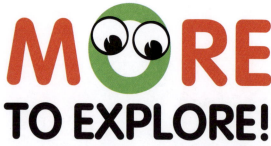

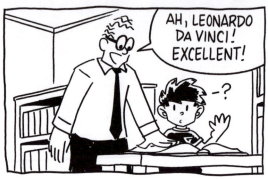

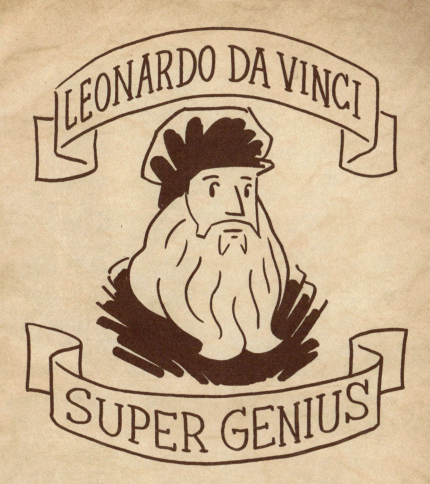

LEONARDO DA VINCI

SUPER GENIUS

The world of G-Man is one of make-believe, so when G-Man references a flying suit designed by the great Renaissance artist and inventor Leonardo da Vinci, it may immediately seem like nonsense made up for a superhero story.

In reality, Leonardo da Vinci REALLY DID create many drawings and designs for wings that would allow a human to fly... as far back as the late 1400s!!!

Leonardo thoroughly studied the construction and mechanics of the wings of birds and bats.

Leonardo applied the mechanical principles of those wings to the design of the ornithopter, a human-powered flight machine! The pilot would turn a crank with foot and hand pedals to make the wings of the ornithopter flap!

Unfortunately, flapping the wings enough to get the ornithopter off the ground would have required more power than a human could generate, something Leonardo would have realized. Hence, he never went beyond the designing stage to actually build a flying machine.

Or DID he?

Leonardo also designed simpler fixed-wing gliders and a parachute that have since been proven to work in our modern era, and COULD have been built with the materials of his day.

This is HIGHLY SPECULATIVE, but there is a VERY SLIGHT CHANCE Leonardo da Vinci MAY have been the world's first REAL superhero!

Leonardo was proficient in map making during a time when maps were so rare that most people had never seen one. He once made a map of the town of Imola and gave it to the town leader.

WOW, THIS MAP IS AWESOME!

HOW DO YOU EVEN KNOW WHAT THE TOWN LOOKS LIKE FROM DIRECTLY ABOVE?

UM... DON'T WORRY ABOUT IT.

Leonardo's designs were centuries ahead of his time, and his genius was not confined to aeronautics. He also created the earliest designs for many other inventions that would not become a reality until hundreds of years later. Here are just a few...

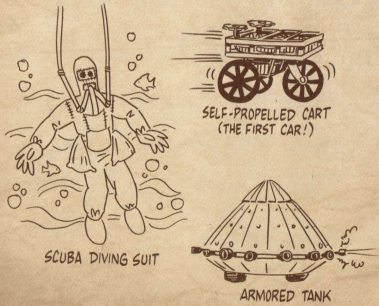

SELF-PROPELLED CART
(THE FIRST CAR!)

SCUBA DIVING SUIT

ARMORED TANK

While many of his more fantastic designs existed only theoretically in drawings, Leonardo actually did build a ROBOTIC KNIGHT — a mechanical suit of armor that could stand, sit, and wave its arms.

He also built a mechanical lion that could walk.

That's right, Leonardo da Vinci was building robots more than 500 years ago. They are now regarded as history's first programmable computers.

As impressive as all of that is, Leonardo is best known for creating the *Mona Lisa*, the most famous painting of all time.

Mona Lisa's mysterious smile has been a source of puzzled fascination for ages. It is as if she is in possession of some secret knowledge that we are now left to merely speculate on. Perhaps it is a secret she shared only with Leonardo.

Mikey is still writing and drawing!

Much more superpowered
excitement is heading your way
in the next volume of...

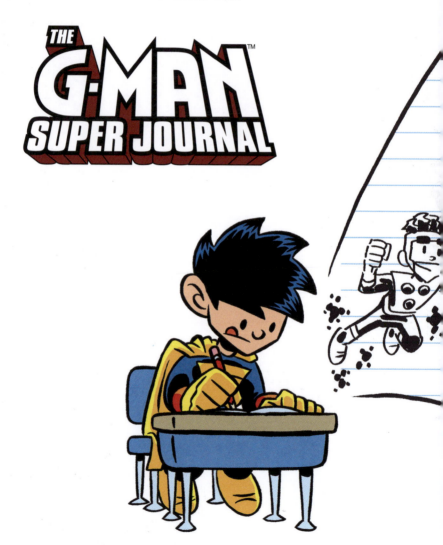

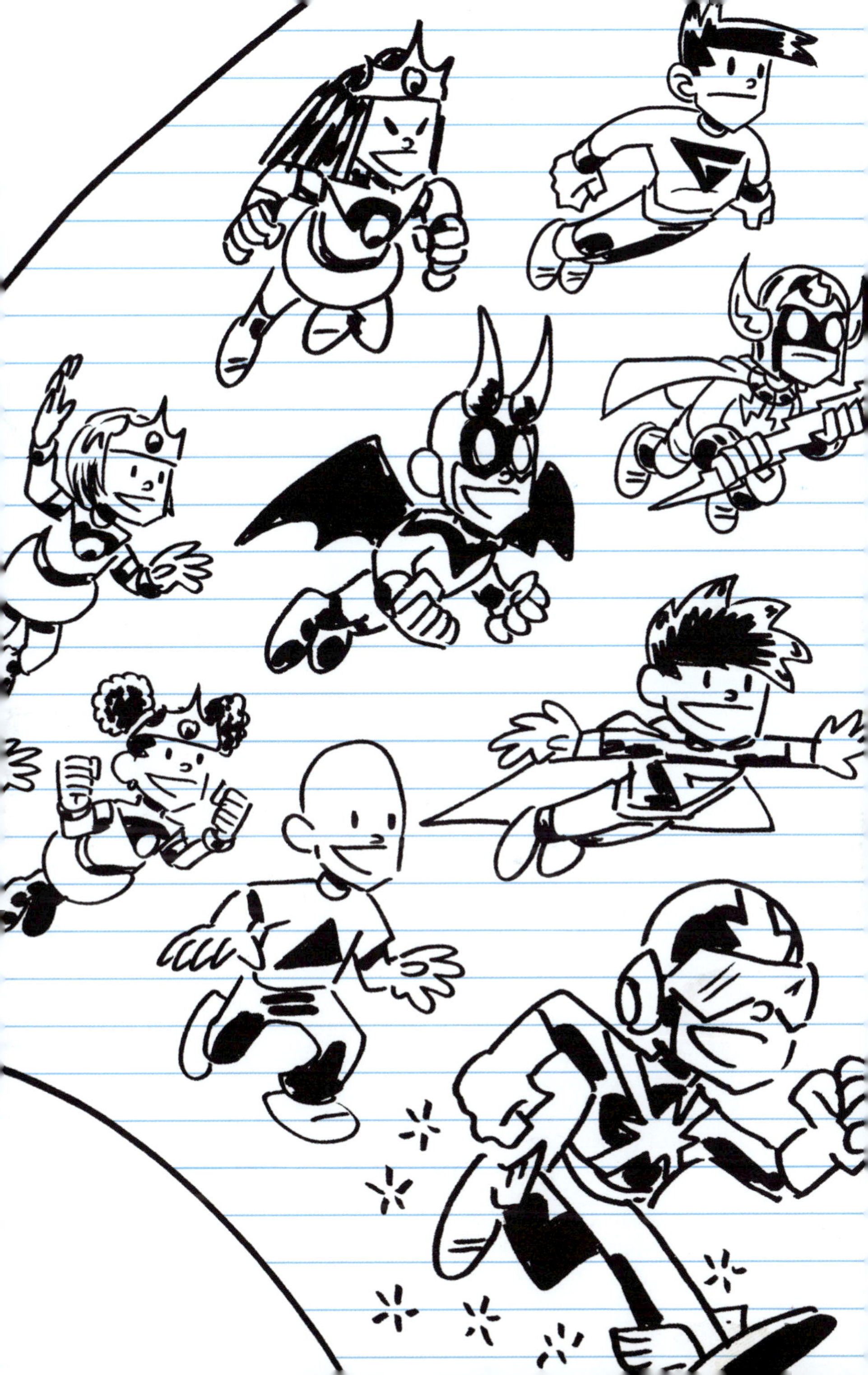

Andrews McMeel Publishing, LLC
an Andrews McMeel Universal company
1130 Walnut Street, Kansas City, Missouri 64106

www.andrewsmcmeel.com

14 15 16 17 18 SDB 10 9 8 7 6 5 4 3 2 1

ISBN: 978-1-4494-5844-7

Library of Congress Control Number: 2014932925

Manufactured by:
Shenzhen Donnelley Printing Company Ltd.
Address and location of manufacturer:
No. 47, Wuhe Nan Road, Bantian Ind. Zone,
Shenzhen China, 518129
1st Printing—12/1/14

ATTENTION: SCHOOLS AND BUSINESSES
Andrews McMeel books are available at quantity discounts with bulk purchase for educational, business, or sales promotional use. For information, please e-mail the Andrews McMeel Publishing Special Sales Department: specialsales@amuniversal.com.

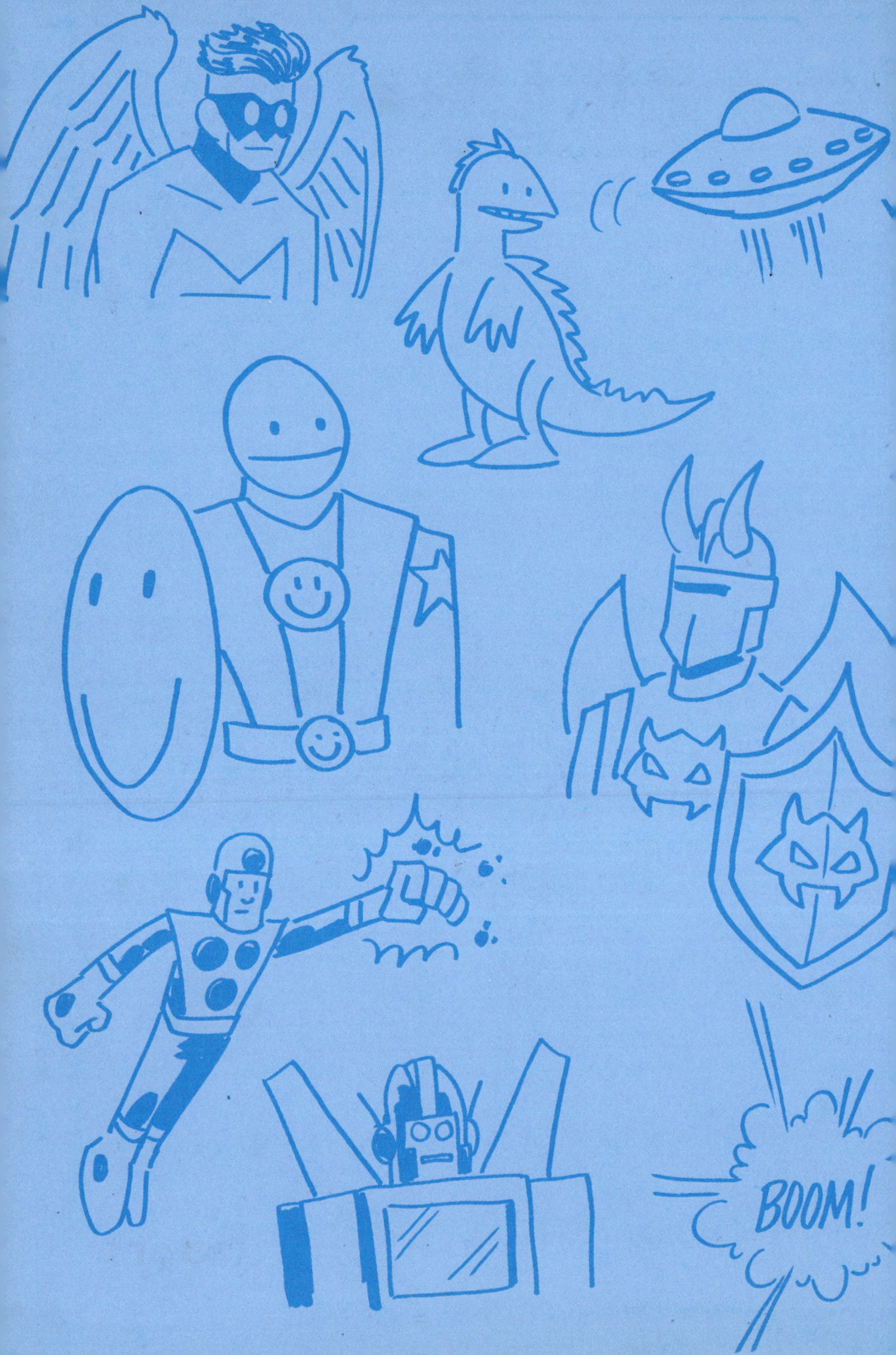
BOOM!